"Kay Dick's mind is a delicate instrument, aware, sensitive, intelligent, alive to every shade of feeling and sensation."
—L. P. Hartley, *Sunday Times*

"The dream setting [of *They*] is cleverly handled, with its shifts of scene and time and its underlying air of menace."
—Mary Sullivan, *Sunday Telegraph*

"[Kay Dick] is a writer who who respects human beings even in their pettiness or confusion; who regards each of them as a worthy object of study and even tenderness, and who devotes as much space and care to the description of what one might call a thoroughly trivial person as to a creature of heroic design."
—Vernon Fane, *The Sphere*

THEY

THEY

A SEQUENCE OF UNEASE

KAY DICK

WITH AN AFTERWORD BY LUCY SCHOLES

McNally Editions

New York

McNally Editions
52 Prince St, New York 10012

Copyright © 1977 by Kay Dick
Afterword © 2021 by Lucy Scholes
All rights reserved
Printed in China
Originally published in 1977 by Allen Lane, London
First McNally Editions paperback, 2022

"Hallo Love" was written in March 1975. An article in the *Sunday Times*, 13 July 1975, "Coping with Grief," described a new psychiatric treatment, a cure designed to relieve bereavement, in which the emotions are "burnt out" and all grief expelled.

Sections of the Afterword appeared originally
in a slightly different form at the *Paris Review Daily* (2020).

ISBN: 978-1-946022-28-8
E-book: 978-1-946022-34-9

Designed by Jonathan D. Lippincott

1   3   5   7   9   10   8   6   4   2

To Judith Burnley and Francis King

CONTENTS

THEY

SOME DANGER AHEAD

Seen through the early September light Karr's house looked magnificent. In fact, it was rather splendid. From his roof there was a full sight of the sea. Karr took me up to give me some bearings. The prospect was that of a narrowing triangle. It could be imagined that Karr lived on an island; a jutting piece of land between two thin rivers, one of which widened as it flowed into the sea, the other a canal, on which some swans floated. Part meadowland, part marshland, with here and there thickets of tall reeds and pockets of sand. A natural bird sanctuary; one was conscious of flight as part of the landscape.

Karr's house was banked up high, walled off, a precaution against flood. Giant hydrangeas, small trees rather than shrubs, were strategically rooted among the oval paving-stones of the terrace; blooms of varying shades of pink sparkled in the autumnal sun, an insolent abundance of flourish, facing south. When we went down to look at them, I could tell that Karr tended them each day. They expressed ritual and care.

'I like the contrast,' I said. Karr understood. He had been standing at the open door at the front of the house as I came up the drive, through the small wood, an oasis in the surrounding estuary.

'That wood was planted long ago,' he said. 'Did you find it difficult to get here?'

'To begin with, yes, but as soon as I reached the old sailors' chapel, I knew I wasn't far off.'

'Did you go in?'

I told him what I had done inside the chapel: opened the Bible at random, closed my eyes and put my finger on one of the pages. The augury game one played in childhood.

'What did you pick?' Karr asked.

'The Revelations of course!' I laughed self-consciously. '*Behold, I come as a thief.*'

'You missed the lodge behind the chapel,' Karr said. 'We'll go over later on.'

The servants were unobtrusive; I hardly noticed their comings and goings. The boy, Jake, introduced his puppy, a black labrador, which reached his chin. 'He's called Omar, after the poet you know.' We sat at the bottom of the austere staircase and told each other stories, until Jake said it was time for Omar's walk.

I joined Karr in the library. The windows opened onto the terrace. 'You can come here as often as you like,' Karr said. He stood at the open window and looked up at the sky. 'Shall we go and see Claire?' he asked.

The ground floor of the lodge had been converted into a studio. I looked at the painting Claire had just finished. It was yellow, all yellow, every variation and depth of yellow. I could hardly bear it. I went outside and rolled on the grass.

'It's beautiful, isn't it?' Karr said.

'Insupportably so.' I went back and looked at it again.

'I'll give it to you if you like,' Claire said.

'Not yet.' I was anxious. 'Not yet.'

'Should I come back with you?' Karr asked.

'I think I shall be quite safe. I'll go across the canal bridge.'

Jake and Omar were waiting for me at the bridge. They waved me off as I veered towards the coast road.

The sun was roughing the skyline over the sea with burnt siena as I reached my cottage. I opened my windows and looked down at the rocks below the cliff. The tide was on the turn. Seagulls were hovering, ready for their last evening catch, as the waves rolled into land again.

I wrote two letters, one to Karr and one to Claire. I went down the sloping track to the beach, and collected some more holed pebbles in the green pools between the rocks. Small crabs ran through my fingers. I made a parcel of three of the stones and addressed them to Jake. *These are sea sculptures and you must name them*, I wrote on a sheet of blue paper.

I decided to go to the village. There was only one stranger sitting on the bench facing the dilapidated jetty. I walked past him twice, but he did not look in my direction. Such news as was, I collected in the shop. 'It's the books at Oxford now.' I nodded as though I was uninterested.

The next day, early, I set out along the beach, walking into the sun. I tested my memory of Keats's poetry. Just after noon, I reached the estuary. I disturbed a colony of butterflies as I clambered up the river bank. Jake and Omar were waiting for me at the top. As we walked towards Karr's house, I told Jake another story, a longer one this time.

'Garth has arrived,' Karr said. 'He's brought his piano.'

'To the chapel?' I asked.

'Yes, he's settled in to remember.' Karr stopped suddenly and looked through his Zeiss Telita at the river. 'You had better stay overnight,' he said.

After lunch I opened the chapel door. Garth sat at the piano staring at the keys. 'It must be possible to remember it all,' he said. 'Given time, yes,' I said, and went out again.

I stopped Jake going in to Garth. 'He is remembering,' I said. 'Later.' Hand in hand we walked to the lodge. Omar bounded after some creature he scented in the wood.

'You don't mind at all do you?' I asked Claire.

'I haven't time to mind,' she said, as she went on painting.

Jake watched her carefully.

'Will you come to Karr's tonight?' I asked.

'I think I might.' She looked at me and kissed me.

The canvas she was painting was blue, all blue, every variation and depth of blue. Jake went outside and cried. Omar licked his tears.

'Let's go and look at the moorhens,' I said to him.

We returned to Karr's house up the steps in the wall onto the terrace. The servants were bringing out tea.

'We'll play chess after dinner,' Karr said, 'until they go to bed.'

'Is Claire in love with Garth?' I asked.

'Aren't we all in love?' Karr smiled at Jake.

'It must be possible . . .' I began.

'To be missed?'

'I suppose that's what I mean.'

'We shall all be reached,' Karr said.

I went to the library and read until dinner. Jake watched me carefully. Karr watered the hydrangeas.

Claire and Garth came in, smiling. He has remembered, I thought, as I caught the defiant look in his eyes. While Karr and I are playing chess, he will make love to Claire in the lodge, and then return to the chapel and play what he remembers. Jake will creep out of bed, and pad like a nocturnal animal to the chapel. He will open the door, close it behind him and listen to Garth carefully. I knew it all as we waited for night.

'You have a new servant.' Claire spoke to Karr.

'Yes. They sent him.' Karr was unperturbed.

'It was to be expected.' Garth looked troubled. 'Should I go away?'

'It is imperative for you to stay,' Karr said.

I woke at dawn, wrote a note to Garth, which I pushed under the chapel door as I passed. On the way back to my cottage I tested my memory of Henry James's later novels. My copy of *Middlemarch* was missing from my bookshelf. I sat in the garden, and thought about Garth remembering the music, and Claire painting, and I stopped being afraid. I made a poem for Jake.

Claire came to see me in the afternoon. She brought a basket filled with blackberries she had picked on the way. Between mouthfuls of berries, we read poems to each other. In every poem some part of our separate lives was contained.

'I don't lock my door any more,' I said. 'They took another book last night.'

'Yes, they're getting more active,' Claire said.

'Their approach is slower in this part of the country,' I said.

'The odd sniper,' Claire laughed.

'The *avant-garde*.' We rocked with hysteria.

'Garth lost everything at once,' Claire said. 'All his scores at once. It's more furtive here.'

I dared the question I most wanted to put. 'Is Jake's memory good enough?'

'Karr has trained him well,' Claire said.

'Will they guess?' I asked.

'Possibly not.' She paused. 'At least, I don't think so, not all at once. With luck, and time, it may be all right.'

'Over-loading?' I had to bring out the fear.

'Not at his age. His memory cells are at their most receptive.' Claire was confident.

As she left I gave her the poem I had written for Jake. I spent the next day swimming and sunbathing, gathering salt and sun into my body, building up my reserves. With my tennis shoes slung round my neck, I paddled out to the breakwater, and watched the fisherman catching shrimps and crabs as the tide ebbed out over the rocks.

'It was London yesterday,' he said. 'They reckon it'll take a week.'

I put on my sunglasses.

'That's quite a catch,' I said, nodding at his bucket.

'Silly buggers,' he said. 'Scurrying under rocks.'

'Some get away,' I said, as he moved to another pool.

Jake and Omar were waiting for me at the cottage.

'Karr said I could stay the night.'

We fed Omar.

'They came when I was waiting outside.' Jake looked worried.

Shelley's poems and Katherine Mansfield's *Journals* were missing. They are getting greedy, I thought. As Jake ate his supper, I told him another story.

'What's a newspaper?' Jake asked.

I slept soundly that night. They never came when one was in the house. In their view confrontation was an unnecessary waste of energy, a luxury they withheld. Silent stealth was a greater pain to bear; it was their form of punishment. They only took sharper measures if one went beyond the accepted limit.

As we crossed the canal bridge leading to Karr's house, we met Garth.

'Karr's new servant, he's watching Claire,' he said.

The fresh canvas was green, all green, every variation and depth of green. Garth turned his face to the wall. Karr's servant left. Claire laughed. I was ready to die for her.

Karr came in. 'You mustn't be over-brave,' he said to Claire. 'It's ostentatious.' He took Jake away from the canvas and walked him towards the wood. Claire sat down and moaned in pain.

'We must go to the house,' I said, 'and order lunch. The servants must be reassured.'

Claire picked some late flowering roses on the way. 'They cleared the National Gallery yesterday,' she said.

During the afternoon Claire went off with Garth. Karr and I sat in the library, which was also a way of loving.

'Garth is reckless,' Karr said. 'Sex makes him reckless.'

I went outside, touched the hydrangeas, sat on the wall and looked over the estuary. I could see Jake flying his kite. Omar bounded after him. Karr's new servant stood on the bridge and watched Jake. A swan stretched its body high above the water and flagged its wings.

'Is Jake safe?' I asked.

'Safety is unimportant,' Karr said.

'But, if he talks?'

'It will be a test.'

It took me four days to overcome my panic. I cleaned my cottage from top to bottom, and dug, planted and pruned in my garden. Five books were missing, including John Stuart Mill's *Autobiography*. I dusted the empty space. The next day it rained. I walked to the village, and on the way I tested my memory of Chekhov's plays. There was a stranger sitting in the café. She asked me to pass her the sugar. Garth came in and sat next to me. 'I can only think about Claire,' he said.

I got up and left. Garth followed me down the street to the beach. We walked back to my cottage along the undercliff.

'Karr expects too much from Jake,' Garth said.

Seagulls screeched. The rain pelted in our faces. As we clambered up the slope to my garden gate, I saw them leaving the cottage. Inside, one whole shelf was denuded of books. In the dust on the wood Garth traced Mahler's name. I brushed my hand over it. I looked out to sea.

'When the rain stops, we'll go to Karr's,' I said.

Garth slept for seven hours. I read Shakespeare's *Sonnets*.

'I've been remembering in my sleep,' Garth said. 'I must find Jake.'

I left Garth at the chapel, went into Karr's house, found Jake, and sent him to Garth.

Karr and I walked slowly to the lodge. A thin mist, a sea fret, cast a webbing over the sun.

'They've got to the coast,' Karr said. 'You could stay here.'

'I don't mind going back,' I said. 'I've conquered my panic.'

Claire was working on a new canvas. It was red, all red, every variation and depth of red. Karr took Claire in his arms.

'I've only one more to paint.' She spoke to Karr rather than to me.

'It could be left,' Karr said in a moment of weakness.

We linked arms as we walked back to the house. The mist had dissolved, and sun glowed on the hydrangeas. The servants brought champagne, and we took our glasses to the terrace wall. Garth and Jake came running towards us, followed by Omar. We looked down over the estuary.

'I will have the yellow canvas now, Claire,' I said. 'I will carry it home.'

'I still have the white to paint,' she said. 'I will do it tonight.'

'That would be foolish,' Karr said.

'I shall write some more letters,' I said.

We turned our backs on the house and looked towards the sea. A trawler was moving from the mouth of the estuary down into the river.

'I think they have finished,' Karr said. 'We can go in now.'

There were no books in the library. We walked slowly through the other rooms in the house. All the paintings had been removed. Claire stroked the spaces where each painting had hung. The servants had left. Garth rushed through the front door. Karr called him to stop. We returned to the terrace and sat in deck chairs. Jake bounced a ball to Omar. Garth returned. He was shaking. 'They've left Claire's paintings,' he said.

'You are not to go back,' Karr said to Claire.

'I must paint the white now,' she said, 'and take Jake with me.'

Some hours later Jake returned.

'You must have your supper and go straight to bed,' Karr said.

We hurried to the lodge. A curlew shrieked. We saw them leading Claire to the trawler roped to the riverbed.

'What will they do to her?' I asked Karr.

'They will blind her, and return her to me,' Karr said. 'She went beyond the accepted limit. She continued to paint.'

Garth raced after them.

'And to him?' I asked.

'They will make him deaf,' Karr said.

'And to me, if?' I was ice all over.

'They would amputate your hands and cut out your tongue,' Karr said. 'You'd better destroy the letters you've written. One must not leave them any possible opening for confrontation.' He paused. 'Think of Jake.'

We went into Claire's studio.

'It's still there,' I said, staring at the white canvas, all white, every variation and depth of white. The other canvases were gone.

'I'll bring Jake to look at it tomorrow morning before they come and take it away,' Karr said.

'It's as white as the sun when you stare into it,' I said.

'One can blind oneself staring at the sun,' Karr said.

'My God!' I said. 'Claire knew, she knew the penalty.'

'We must all know that,' Karr said. 'It's the only certainty we have.'

As we returned to the house Karr said, 'All your books would now have been taken. There is no point in your going back.'

'There's paper and pens under the floorboards,' I said.

'They must stay there,' Karr said.

'For Jake?' I asked.

'Perhaps, perhaps not,' Karr paused. 'I will find him a companion of his own age, just in case.'

'In case they get onto Jake?' I asked.

'Yes,' said Karr. 'There is very little time left.'

THE VISITANTS

I was the first to see them.

'It's just possible,' Sandy had said, 'they might miss us. We offer few attractions.'

It was too late to turn back. I faced the sun as I walked towards them. There were nine of them on the beach. Three breakwaters along Sandy was painting his boat. Eight of them were stretched out on the shingle. The ninth was crouched on his knees, looking in Sandy's direction. My dog barked at them. It was the first day of Spring. The sun was warm water on the skin, and the sea a still silver curving horizon. A cormorant dived in and out of the water, frivolously almost. As I passed them I smiled; it was best to do so. One of them stood up and waded into the waves, fully clothed, up to his waist. One of the girls laughed.

'I'll give it another coat tomorrow.' Sandy patted his boat.

'Will you go away?' I asked.

'I'd rather not.' He packed up his tackle. 'Let's have tea at Judith's.'

Berg was working in the conservatory. He waved. Judith's mother was playing patience in her usual window corner in the drawing-room. The boys were making a yellow and blue kite. Sandy offered to help. The Italian girl came in carrying a tea tray, followed by Judith. The Siamese cat spat at my dog.

'Three of them came to the kitchen door this afternoon,' Judith said. 'Cook gave them some cakes and fruit.'

'I used to know Yeats,' Judith's mother said.

'We'll test the kite tomorrow.' The younger boy lifted it high for us to see.

'I hope it keeps fine.' Judith was anxious. 'They might move on.'

'They're probably only passing through.' Sandy sounded casual.

'They asked Cook how many people lived here.' Judith was still uneasy.

'You're a family unit. That should satisfy them.' Sandy fastened another cord to the kite.

'It's you two I'm worried about,' Judith said.

The telephone rang. We heard Berg answer it. The boys went out to the garden.

'They're prospecting,' Berg said, as he came into the room. 'The usual tactics.'

Living alone was not at first easy. Acclimatization was gradual. Once accepted, the benefits were there to be savoured. It had taken me years to understand how to use them. I thought about this as Sandy and I walked back to my cottage.

'You've always lived alone, haven't you?' I asked.

'Yes. Friends come to stay. That's stimulating, and keeps me going.'

'One needs one's own time,' I said.

'Essential.' Sandy was definite.

I knew exactly what he meant. There was no wind, almost a motionless evening. Sound has a penetrable quality at such times. We heard them laugh as we came nearer the beach.

'Sometimes, I envy Judith,' I said.

'The family?' It was more statement than question.

'Yes, but . . .'

'Not all the time, I think.'

'Good to have them near—available.'

'Not encroaching.'

Sandy stayed to supper. We talked until one in the morning.

'You're not worried, are you?' He hesitated.

'Not at all.' I laughed. 'I can always phone you.'

'They're arbitrary. They may have gone by morning.' Sandy wished me good night.

'I think,' Judith said, as I was making coffee the next morning, 'that you'd be wise to stay with us for a few days.'

'That would be panicky,' I said.

'There are more of them, coming I mean,' Judith said. 'Berg heard there was havoc further inland. No singles were spared.'

'Unusual.' I tried to appear calm. 'They're not so thorough. A few are always by-passed.'

I went for my walk with the dog in the afternoon, deliberately making for the beach. It was better not to betray apprehension. They had moved a little further westwards, nearer Sandy, who was working on his boat. I nodded as

I passed them. One of them threw a pebble into the sea. Sandy took me to his place for tea.

'They left this outside my door.' He showed me a crucifix made of seaweed.

He took me to his workshop. We looked at his latest glass sculpture. I was dazzled by its beauty.

I rested my head on his chest. The thunder was unexpected. Light faded. Lightning flashed. The storm lasted an hour.

'They'll be drenched,' I said.

'They don't mind,' Sandy said.

We looked out to sea. The sun shone again. Soft pinks shaded the now quiet waves, the breakwaters acquired a new dimension. The unfinished jetty looked magnificent, like some prehistoric object of immense solidity. It was a breathtaking sight. As I walked home I saw smoke rising from the beach.

I pottered in my garden until the light faded. Indoors, I studied an ordnance map of our part of the coast. In red pencil I crossed the places where they had left their mark. I linked the crosses together in blue ink; it made an incomplete circle. I finished the circle in pencil. We were, fractionally, off their course.

I telephoned Sandy. 'We're not in their circle.' I explained my findings.

'Don't forget, circles begin within circles.' He sounded amused.

'You mean we may be the beginning of a new one?'

'Possible, unless . . .'

'Unless?'

'Unless they're a breakaway group. That does happen.'

'You mean freelancing?'

'Well,' he laughed, 'say singles operating together. Berg would know; he's working on a social study of their behaviour patterns. For the future of course.'

'Ah yes, for the future. Sandy,' I was sharp, 'what do you mean they're singles?'

'Well, Berg says that when singles are dispossessed, they often link up.'

'Because of loneliness?'

'Yes, it makes for easier living.'

'They give in?'

'Let's say they give up being active singles.'

'Would you give up, Sandy?'

He laughed again. 'No, I'm a dedicated single.'

'Even if . . . ?' I feared to mention it.

'All is destroyed?' He took up the challenge. 'Destruction doesn't count. One can always create again.'

Would one, I wondered, as I replaced the receiver and looked at my books. Was not this evidence a spur? Without it, would one continue? How much did one rely on past achievement? It could be a test, if destruction came. They were very thorough once they selected a target. Berg said their passivity was internal combustion working outwards to finite action. I thrust the panic from me, and worked until I was dead tired. It was no good listening for footsteps; they wore no shoes.

I was having breakfast in the garden when Berg came. I made him some coffee. He smoked one of the Lārranagas he usually reserved for the afternoon. I tried to delay his news which I somehow anticipated.

'Sandy's?' I asked. 'When?'

'Between three and four in the morning,' Berg said.

'Sandy?'

'He put up a fight.'

'Dear God!' I poured more coffee into Berg's cup.

'In hospital,' Berg said. 'They used some of his glass to his eyes. I'd always told him it would be of no use.' Berg sounded cross. 'Best always to walk away. They only attack the individual if a stand is made.'

'We must go over,' I said.

It was the workshop. An absolute shambles. I picked up my dog in case he cut himself on the shattered pieces. Sandy's acid had been poured over all his sketches. A sea of glass pebbles. The blues, reds, yellows and greens of Sandy's designs were mashed together—a madman's palate of colour.

'And if Sandy had lived with me, or in your house? This wouldn't have happened?' It was a question to Berg, although I knew the answer. 'Why?'

'The single is a menace to them,' Berg said. 'They fear solitary living, therefore envy it.'

'But they hardly speak to each other.'

'They have reduced speech to a minimum, to such an extent that they can barely articulate their words.'

I remembered how they began, a parody for the newspapers. No one wrote about them now. That was too dangerous. They were an ever-possible encounter. A potential menace one had to live with.

'How many are there?' I asked Berg.

'Over a million, nearer two, I suspect. There's no way of telling exactly.' Berg kicked at the glass. 'You should marry Sandy,' he added, 'or, at least, live together.'

Judith drove me to the hospital. Sandy's eyes were bandaged. So were his hands. I made him the offer Berg had suggested.

'I haven't come so far to retreat now,' he said.

'You must stop being obstinate. Both of you.' Judith was upset. 'There's no point in bravado. You could continue working without fear if you lived together.'

'A matter of choice,' Sandy said. 'If we lack choice we lack everything.'

On the drive back Judith became insistent. 'You must protect yourself. If it's not this group, it'll be another.'

'There's always danger, somewhere, in living,' I said. 'Drop me here. I'll walk the rest of the way. I need to think—by myself.'

Near the beach I met Judith's mother.

'I told them I knew Yeats,' she said, as she passed me without stopping. I looked up at the blue and yellow kite the boys were flying for the first time.

Two of them were standing at my garden gate. My dog barked.

'Good afternoon,' I smiled at them.

'You a loner?' the man asked.

'I live with my dog,' I said.

'Jed,' he introduced himself.

'Lou,' she said.

I invited them in to tea. They ate bread and butter with honey and seedcake. They followed me round the cottage and looked at everything. I took them out to the garden and showed them my flowers, shrubs and fruit. They did not speak. My dog stopped barking at them. I offered them cigarettes, which they refused. They sat on the grass, and

I went indoors to wash up the tea things. When I went out again, I saw Jed take off his brass necklace and string it round my dog's neck. He pulled the chain tighter. I stopped myself rushing forward, and walked slowly. 'He trusts you,' I said. Jed loosened his hold.

'I must give him his supper.' I felt the sweat dripping from my armpits. Jed let the chain drop from the dog's neck.

I walked back to the kitchen, followed by the dog and Lou. I cut up some meat. Lou watched me give it to the dog. 'I must write a few letters,' I said. Lou sat on the floor and watched me. At seven o'clock, I told Lou to tell Jed we would have supper. They watched me boil eggs, prepare a salad and set the food on the table. As we ate, I talked about my garden. 'I like flowers,' Lou said. Jed slapped her face.

After supper I arranged the chess pieces on the board. Jed and I played three games. I lost two. Lou walked outside with the dog in the garden.

Berg called.

'You live here?' Jed asked.

Berg hesitated.

'No,' I said firmly.

Berg played a game with Jed. It lasted two hours. I sat in the garden with Lou. I picked her a long spray of white lilac. Jed stalked out, snatched it from her and threw it away. The dog played with it. Lou spat in Jed's face. Jed returned to the chess game with Berg. It finished in a draw.

'I will stay here tonight if you like,' said Berg.

'Thank you but,' I made my voice sound very clear, 'Lou and Jed are staying here tonight.'

'Right,' Jed said.

Berg left. There was a smell of fish coming from the sea: that meant rain. 'I'll make some hot drinks,' I said as we went into the house and closed the door. Lou pulled the curtains. Jed moved the lamp so that it shone directly onto the curtains. My dog barked. Jed placed his hand over its mouth.

I felt them rather than heard them. The garden gate creaked as they opened it. Jed pushed the dog towards me. I covered its head with my sweater to stop it barking. I heard them now. Damp naked footsteps on the path. Jed grabbed Lou. Between the lamp and the curtained window, he pawed at her in a mock love-making. The slithery padding outside stopped. Then it started up again. I closed my eyes, expecting to hear the door open. I heard the garden gate creak again. Then silence. I opened my eyes. Jed pushed Lou away from him. She fell onto the sofa and went to sleep.

'You trust us,' Jed said, as he rearranged the chess pieces on the board and began to replay the game he drew with Berg. I sat and watched him, and listened as the rain started.

I woke about six. I was stiff from sleeping in the armchair. Jed and Lou had gone. The curtains were drawn back from the window. I went outside. Lilac sprays, on the garden table, were arranged in a completed circle. For me, for the time being, there would be another interlude of safety. I ran to the beach, followed by my dog.

Judith's mother, on her usual morning walk, half-paused as we met.

'I saw them go,' she chanted. 'I told them I used to know Yeats.'

POCKET OF QUIETUDE

'I have come a long way to see you,' I said to Hurst. 'I went to Cumberland, but you'd left.'

'I thought I'd come home,' he said, as he led me to the mill.

I paused on the bridge, and looked at the water spinning through the mill's wheel.

'I'm very tired,' I said.

'The sound of water will help you sleep tonight.' Hurst left the door open as we went inside. The red floor stones were cool to the feet. I touched one of the thick oak beams. All the windows were open; the sun reached every corner. Tea was laid: boiled eggs and a comb of honey.

'It's everywhere, isn't it?' *Die schöne Müllerin* music came to mind.

Hurst understood. 'There are three interlinking canals. The weir borders one side of the garden. Almost an island home.'

'Space and light, you've filtered them into every room.' I walked round Hurst's converted mill. Each room connected with another. 'And echoes,' I added, listening to the water outside.

'Look, there's the kingfisher.' Hurst nodded at a window.

I saw a flash of blue-green wing and rusty breast.

In the gallery room the top branches of surrounding trees were visible from each of the eight windows. One of Hurst's mandalas hung from a wooden beam, and a mobile swayed in motion with the breeze coming from outside. I climbed the ladder to the gallery.

'There's another way down. All my entrances are exits,' Hurst said. 'It makes for completion.'

I appreciated his planning. 'And you can see every corner of the landscape.'

Hurst laughed. 'It has its uses as a watch-tower.'

In the distance I saw the smoke. 'They're burning again,' I said.

'That's why my water is useful. Now, I have an efficient fire-extinguishing unit. It switches itself on when I touch the control key. I'd better show you where that is—as a precaution.'

'Are these some of Julian's paintings?' I looked at the walls.

'Most of them are his.'

The mill belonged to Hurst. For five years Julian had lived here with his wife and the twins. After the burning Julian's wife took the children to Switzerland. Hurst spent a year travelling round the country, visiting what he called the pockets of quietude, retreats like the mill for those who were not acquiescent.

'I saved the mill, but could do nothing to help Julian.' Julian had been Hurst's only son. 'I built my workshop on the spot.'

We went into the garden, over the bridge of the first canal. Outside the workshop was a charred block of wood. On it were carved Julian's name and occupation—painter. There were no dates of birth or death. A boat was tied to one of the canal banks.

'I'll attend to your roses,' I said; it was important to plan for the future. Any attempt to give up was playing into their hands. Inaction was what they wanted. I walked round the garden and climbed up to the tree-house Julian had built for the twins. Hurst, inside the mill, switched on the lights. From the garden, surrounded by water, it looked like a squat ship in harbour. I felt I was being watched from the other side of the weir. I waved to the face I saw peering, pressed against one of the gallery windows now closed. Then I saw Hurst standing on the bridge.

'Who else has come?' I felt cold.

'No one yet,' Hurst said as we went indoors.

'I must have imagined the face,' I explained to Hurst.

'The reflection of a passing owl probably.' Hurst sounded easy.

'Hurst,' I determined to make the admission, 'I'm frightened.'

'Of course,' he said. 'We're all frightened. We must live with it. Russell and Jane will be here tomorrow. They got through London. I'll be sleeping in the room opposite yours tonight. You are over-tired; it's the strain.'

I went into the study and borrowed a Conrad for the night. There was every book I had once owned, and many thousands more. A photograph of Julian stood on the desk. The bearded young face was smiling. I dozed rather than slept that night. Although I had drawn back the curtains the darkness outside was menacing. Apprehension filled the room. I heard Hurst moving about; a beam of light showed through the communicating door. When dawn came, I told myself that my inner tension, relaxing at long last, had produced these uneasy night fears, overlaps from childhood.

Russell came in with my breakfast.

'Jane's asleep; we arrived about five this morning.'

He looked younger than I remembered. 'Dear, dear Russell,' I said, 'I'm so glad you've come through.'

'I'm a cunning chap,' he grinned. 'I walk through fire, didn't you know?'

'No, please.' I shut my eyes remembering the fire. I had watched them as methodically they went to work on my home.

'One must never forget,' Russell said. 'I hold it in mind all the time. That way I'm continually on the lookout. It helps me move more quickly, knowing danger is there. It's when you try and forget that trouble begins. That's the way they approach, through the unguarded moment.'

'You mean I must remember?'

'Every single detail. What you know becomes a protection.'

As I went downstairs, through the gallery room, Russell was playing Bach on Hurst's upright Blüthner. Hurst came out of his workshop. 'Want to come with me to the village? I'm collecting some stores. You mustn't try and work yet. Just let the tiredness ease out.'

The village, sited on a hill, commanded a view of the whole weald. The September day was gloriously warm. Greetings were given to Hurst all along the main street.

'Why are you so protected?' I asked.

'I'm the miller, didn't you know?' He smiled. 'Symbolically, of course. I harbour the life-force—the grain.'

A woman of middle age walked into the pond, disturbing the ducks. She shook herself like a dog as she emerged from the water, stopped in front of us, and spat at Hurst. He gave her some money. Three boys followed her for a while, jeering at her, as she zigzagged towards the church.

'Hurst, that wasn't?' I could hardly speak.

'Yes, it was,' he said. 'Her children's books were too full of fantasy for them to leave her alone.'

'Shouldn't we have?' I hardly knew what it was we should have done.

'Nothing,' Hurst said. 'She camps in the church with some of the others. She remembers little, except possibly the fire, which is why she walks into the pond every morning, to extinguish what memory remains. She is no threat to them now.'

The scene in Hurst's garden on our return was oddly foreign: lunch laid out on a rectangular wooden table. A festive sight, like some memory from childhood.

'Oh Jane!' I greeted her, careful not to look at her right arm.

'I'm writing poetry again.' Her voice was joyous.

'A proper dab with her left arm now.' Russell kissed her. 'What a smashing clever wife I have.'

'Actually, I think my left hand is rather more creative.' It was a boast.

When they threw Jane's poetry into the fire, instinctively, she had rushed forward: they held her right arm over the flames for eight minutes. Russell had acted differently.

'You've forgotten this,' he had said as he hurled his recently finished fugue into the fire.

After lunch Hurst suggested a walk. I felt lazy and decided to remain behind. 'I'll have tea ready for you when you come back,' I said.

I set about clearing the table, carrying the things into the mill. I washed up and laid tea indoors. I went upstairs to wash. Then, dreamily, I moved through the upper rooms. The mill's identity was a living presence. It was all so beautiful; every object a link to the next one. I was preternaturally conscious of the books, the paintings, the music, and the tops of the trees seen through every window. All the windows were open and water plashed through my ear-drums. Then it came over me, a damp cold sweat, attacking my shoulders and running down my spine. I was immobilized by an unseen threat. My back was against one of the open windows. I looked up at the gallery. There was nothing there. Then I heard the crash, above my head. I went up the ladder. An unreal stillness made me hesitate before walking through to the adjoining room. It was a painting that had fallen down. I picked it up and stood it against the wall. I walked slowly through all the other rooms, and came down again by the staircase into the gallery room. I stopped myself from rushing. I went downstairs and out into the garden. Standing on the bridge I knew I had been followed. I looked up at every window in turn. One of them was now closed. I sat in a deck chair facing the mill for about thirty minutes. Then I regained my equanimity, went to the tool shed, found the secateurs, and started dead-heading the roses.

After dinner we took our coffee and wine up to the gallery room. Hurst closed all the windows. We talked about old times and friends we shared. It was so low a sound that first I thought I had imagined it. Russell stood up and listened.

'They're taking the boat away,' Hurst said. 'They do that periodically. Then they return it. I make a point of not noticing either way.'

'Why?' I asked.

'A petty intimation of their permanent presence.' Hurst looked out. 'Yes, it's gone.' He half-laughed. 'We can be assured of a peaceful night.'

'But this is a very large house, many rooms in this mill.' My voice was thin.

'Every three hours I walk through all the rooms,' Hurst said.

'Wouldn't they know that?' asked Jane.

'They'd anticipate some vigilance,' Hurst replied.

'Where's Russell?' Jane was tense.

We started to rush about. Hurst stopped us. 'We must look for him together.' It did not occur to any of us to shout out his name. Downstairs we found the front door open. Russell was standing on the bridge. Jane ran to him. He held her tightly. 'It's all right,' he said. 'Only a shadow cast by the fig tree.'

'Hurst.' I grabbed his arm. 'Wouldn't it be better to confront them?'

'It's a matter of survival, not of suicide.' He smiled. 'The pockets are increasing. This is passive resistance positively demonstrated. The effect will be accumulative.'

'Have we the patience, let alone the nerves to last it out?' I was near hysteria.

'We may not last it out, but we must do it as creatively as there is time left.'

'Aren't we keeping dead tombs alive?'

'Yes, tombs full of treasure, like this mill.' His tone was almost smug. 'Keepers, if you like.' He lit his pipe. 'Don't forget I'm the miller. We can all add to the treasure, however short the time left may be. It can't all be destroyed. Some of it will remain for those who come after us.'

'I don't feel at all brave, Hurst. I'd rather make a stand, face them.'

'A waste of creative energy,' he said. 'Remember what happened when you did that.'

'But I didn't fight. I just stood and watched them destroy.'

'They let you go. You were lucky, and so were Jane and Russell.'

I reminded him that they had not let Julian go.

'Learn to conquer fear,' Hurst said.

'But it's everywhere.' I was near breaking-point. 'In this mill. I know it's here.'

'Yes, it's here. One can live with it, though. One must. I intend to. Come on, let's make some fresh coffee.' We went indoors and back to the gallery room.

'We will all work tomorrow,' Jane said. 'You will feel stronger then.'

'I don't think I can work again,' I said. Then I saw him, looking down at us from the gallery.

'Good evening, Hurst,' he said, as he came down the ladder. 'You have guests again I see.'

'Some coffee?' Hurst was remote.

'Thank you, no, I'm just going.' He looked at each of us in turn. 'Let me not disturb you. Merely a routine inspection.' His eyes glanced at Jane's right arm. 'You've come through London, I hear?'

'It was on our way.' Russell spoke calmly.

'Unfortunate destruction of course, yet necessary. We shall have to build again. An open-plan style this time. Better community facilities. No self-contained units.'

'Indeed, we shall build again,' Russell challenged him.

'Pity about your music,' he said. 'I rather enjoyed it. Now I mustn't take up more of your time together. Don't bother to see me out, Hurst; I know the way.'

We heard the door bang as he left.

'Was that a warning?' Jane asked.

'I rather think so,' Hurst said.

We heard a car start up and move off. We listened until the sound of its engine was lost in the distance.

'Can we go on like this?' I asked.

'Oh yes,' Jane said, 'we can go on even better now. There is no option.'

'What about some cheerful tunes?' Russell seated himself at the piano and spun out a medley of old sentimental numbers. Hurst poured out more wine. Jane and I sang the words. We went to bed relaxed of tension.

For nine days we each of us worked in our own way, stimulating each other with our renewed energy. Pressure lent power and speed to our production. The boat was returned and tied to the bank again. Between bouts of work we played chess, gardened, read, listened to music, and swam in the canals. We agreed not to walk beyond Hurst's land. The weather changed. Rain kept us indoors. We played table tennis in what had once been the twins' playroom.

'Can we go on creating for ourselves? Without any contact with the outside world?' I asked Jane as she watched me play a complicated game of patience.

'The question of the ages.' Then, softly, she said, 'I think they're here again.'

Hurst and Russell were playing chess.

'How do you know?' I tidied my cards.

She went over to the window. 'There are three of them. One for each of us,' she said.

'But, we're four, with Hurst,' I said.

'Three without,' Jane said.

I felt no fear. 'Should we try and move on or stay?' I asked.

'We'll stay.' Jane was definite.

I joined her at the window. 'They look rather small seen from here,' I said. 'Does Hurst know?'

Jane looked at me. 'He sent for them. Haven't you guessed his role? The miller?'

A moment of clarity came to me. 'Of course!' I said. 'And we walked into the ivory tower. We're his hostages, not to fortune.' I wanted to laugh. 'Hostages to the dead, to Julian.' Something else occurred to me: 'Did you know this when you came?'

'I knew,' Jane said. 'I told Russell. He didn't think it important.'

'It's irrational,' I protested.

'Not at all. A rational bargain. He keeps our work. They have us. In that way Hurst's treasures are safe.'

'And we add to them?'

'You might say that Hurst gives us the possibility of adding to them.'

'And there'll be other guests after us?'

'Naturally, the tomb must ever be enriched.'

'Keeper of the grain.' I remembered Hurst's imagery. 'But he's fond of us.'

'Oh, he loves us. We are extensions of what Julian stood for.'

I shuddered at a thought. 'You mean he . . . ?'

'Well, he saved the mill, not Julian.'

'Check.' Hurst's voice rasped out. He stood up. 'I'm glad you've worked it out for yourselves. Less to explain. I was almost certain you'd reach the logical conclusion.'

'And when do they come for you, Hurst?' asked Russell.

'When I am dead, they will replace me.' He walked away from us down the stairs. We heard him open the front door.

Russell opened the windows. It had stopped raining.

'Hallo darling.' Jane gave her left hand to Russell.

We heard them coming up the stairs.

PEBBLE OF UNEASE

The January day had the pellucidity of a crystal. Unseasonable sun transformed the landscape. Winter bleakness acquired definition. Following weeks of rain the sharpness was invigorating. Downlands radiated colour. Brownish defoliated areas glinted purple tones. Leafless bramble and thicket sparkled with renewal of bud. Sodden lumps of green turf felt like moss under my tread. I looked at the cerulean blue of the sky framing curves and inclines. It was good to be alive. My dog dug at one of the burrows, scenting creatures in hibernation. I breathed deeply, and walked slowly towards the highest peak. A lark chirruped above my head, flew rapidly upwards and, wings outstretched, dropped vertically without sound into a nosedive. I whistled my appreciation. The lark repeated the acrobatic feat.

At a bend in the narrow track I met the old man and his scraggy terrier. 'A fair round day,' he said, as he stood aside to let me pass. Our dogs sported a joust. I could see the village and the football pitch. Blue and red jerseyed figures raced between the goal-nets.

At the top I looked down at the sea, a map of tranquillity. Paths of golden sun stretched from shore rocks to the sky's horizon. In childhood one believed it possible to run through these illusionary lanes. I glanced back for a sight of the old man. I watched him descend. He stumbled and fell. I started to run back towards him, but he picked himself up, went on, less chirpily, his terrier close to his heels. Then I saw them, standing on the top of the opposite ridge. A column of them in line, each one holding a pole to match his height. With deliberate precision they broke formation, gyrated downwards, executing a pattern of zigzagging motions, crossing and recrossing one another's steps, until they reached the bottom. It was an exercise. I heard the lark warbling again but did not look up.

Concentrating hard on the crisp winter afternoon, I made my way to the Old Rectory situated in the last hollow of the downs.

'Hallo,' Julian said. 'You're in time for tea.'

Fion rushed to greet me, followed by Mutley, his shaggy sheepdog, who immediately rounded up my dog and, without touching him, drove him back into the garden.

'My tortoise has woken up,' Fion said. 'Come and see him.' He put his small hand in mine.

'Later, Fion,' said Olwen, holding a plate of scones in one hand; she pushed the boy towards the drawing-room.

After tea I told them about the exercise and the old man falling.

'The rites of spring—premature, invoking the old man's primitive superstitions; thus the fall, a sort of reverential awe,' Julian said.

'Darling,' Olwen said, 'we're not your pupils. Stop the rationale.'

'Mutley would have rounded them up.' Fion was excited.

Breaking the tension I said to Fion: 'Show me your tortoise.'

'I don't like school so much this term.' Fion tucked more straw round the small carapace in the cardboard box. 'Everyone's so cross. And there aren't any secrets.'

'Secrets?' I smiled at him.

'I haven't any best friend any more. No one wants to listen to secrets. I'm awfully good at secrets. I have to tell them to Mutley now.' Fion sighed. 'I do miss a best friend.'

I stayed to supper. Later Julian offered to drive me home.

'Don't forget,' Olwen said as she kissed me good-bye, 'you can always come to us.'

'Are you worried, Julian?' I asked in the car.

'Sniffing the air you might say. Not more than that. It's all too vague, as yet.' He rubbed his window clear of condensation. 'I've nothing to complain about, except details. Some cuts, more suggestions than directions. It's the students who disturb me. Yet, here again, nothing positive to pick on. A general lethargy, unusual at the start of a new term.'

We drove on in silence. The night was star-spattered. Bright, slightly frosty. Some bobbing lights at sea indicated fishing trawlers.

'You've a good view from here.' Julian looked towards the sea as he stopped outside my cottage.

The terrace had a friendly air. Lights still on in several rooms. My garden was clearly defined in the strong moonlight. I noted more bulbs sprouting through before their time and fresh shoots on the shrubs. My neighbour, David, was standing outside my front door. For one moment I failed to recognize him. He waved a milk jug at me. 'I've run out,' he said.

I let us both in, poured milk into his jug and offered him some tea which he accepted. We chatted trivialities and praised the change in the weather. I gave him opportunities to tell me why he was waiting for me to return home, but he ignored them all. After he left I felt suddenly tired. The fine day was premature, and oddly inappropriate. My telephone rang. It was David. 'I forgot to tell you,' he said. 'That old man with the shaggy dog. He died.' 'I'm sorry,' I said. 'Heart attack probably. Near the football pitch.' He'd been walking on the downs.' 'His dog?' I asked. 'It ran away.' 'Unusual!' I said.

I attempted to work. I wrote two pages and tore them up. Outside someone screamed. I rushed out. Mary, my other neighbour, was standing at my gate. She was pointing downwards. It was the old man's terrier, dead. I shooed my dog out of the way, bent down and touched the body. It was still warm. Its neck was broken.

'Why put it here?' Mary asked when I calmed her down.

I left her question unanswered. She watched me fetch a sack, tuck it round the dead animal and carry the body into the garden shed. 'I'll get the vet to remove him tomorrow,' I said. I wondered what I had seen that afternoon and not noticed.

'Very professional,' the vet said, as he inspected the dead dog. 'At least it didn't suffer. One snap, and that was it. Nasty leaving it outside your gate.' He paused. 'Some lout I suppose. I heard the old man died yesterday. Just as well. He'd have broken his heart over this.'

'They said the dog ran away.'

'Surprising that,' the vet said.

'That's what I thought.'

'So much cruelty today—towards animals I mean.' The vet washed his hands. 'Quite mindless.'

'I wonder,' I said, 'whether it is mindless.'

'Well,' the vet was at the door. 'Must be getting on. Another fine day. Colder though.'

I watched him carry the sack to the boot of his estate van. I returned to the downs in the afternoon. The wind drew tears from my eyes. I put on my dark glasses for protection; they also had the virtue of optical lenses. Clouds obscured the sun. Just beyond the football pitch, at the beginning of the track leading over the hill was a large notice: *Danger. Exercise practice.* I turned back and went home along the cliff road. The sea was green and looked icy cold. Gulls swirled round and round, a restless excursion into land and back to sea. Olwen was sitting in her car outside my cottage.

Indoors I told her the news about the old man and his dog.

'Forget about it,' she said. 'Best not to notice these things.'

I expressed surprise.

'One starts adding up. Julian's doing it all the time. Little things, irrelevancies, omissions, contradictions, ambiguities. He's forever searching for reasons. And the reasons don't satisfy. They can't, because they don't fit. His students don't borrow his books any more, so he gets in a fret. He probes and questions. They just stare at him.'

'And that doesn't upset you?'

'I tell him to use his energy for his own work, and for us. Fion has begun to be puzzled. I encourage him to talk it out in fantasy. At school they stop him now, or rather he finds there is no audience for his stories.'

'You are saying that . . .' I began.

'I'm saying nothing except that one must not notice these . . .'

'Pointers?' I finished her sentence.

'If you like.' Her green eyes flashed irritation. 'It's contagious.'

'We must remain healthy?' I used the adjective ironically.

'In control,' Olwen said, then more lightly: 'Keep our cool.'

'Yet there are mysteries?' I ventured. 'The old man and his dog?'

'Rubbish! Coincidence of accidents; one natural, the other mindless.' She used the vet's word.

'Surely, Olwen, you and I can exchange secrets? I mean the truth?'

'We don't need to. We know them. Let them lie quiet.'

I pushed her a little further. 'Acquiescent, then?'

'Passive resistance.' Olwen's voice was high.

'Ignorance is bliss, you're saying?'

'Damn you,' she said. 'I've two people to worry about.'

'Ah yes, sorry,' I said. 'I've only my own preoccupations.'

She held out her hand. I took it.

'They want us to be anxious,' she said.

We returned to the commonplaces of conversation.

'Should you ever,' Olwen hesitated as she got into her car, 'ever wish for a change, don't forget the Old Rectory. We're not too far away.'

'I won't.' I waved her off.

Later David returned the borrowed milk. I understood this to mean he wanted a chat. I gave him a drink.

'You're lucky,' he said, 'working at home. Not having to deal with other people.'

I did not contradict him.

'I'm in an absolute frazzle!' he said. 'Nothing goes right, yet nothing goes really wrong. I mean to say if one could close the door between work and leisure, if you see what I mean. Now that's not possible. The journey home is sheer murder. Sullen faces, scowls, and of course, one never knows what to expect.' He accepted another drink. 'I came here to escape, the pressure I mean. This is a safe area.'

'It's comparatively safe.' I tried to reassure him.

As I moved to pour him out a third drink I saw the ambulance draw up and stop outside Mary's house. David and I went out, quickly, ready to help. They opened the back door. A nurse ushered Mary out. Mary's face was blank; she did not acknowledge us.

'What's happened?' I asked.

'She's disorientated.' The driver was curt.

We went back inside without a word. We knew only too well what that meant. For a day or two they would come and care for her. After that she would be taken away. It was a common disease, officially cited as incurable.

'I wonder who our new neighbour will be,' David said. It was factual rather than callous.

The rain set in for two weeks. At night I heard foghorns. The new neighbour was a young man. David attempted to strike up an acquaintanceship, but failed. My attempts were no more successful. He went out at nine in the morning and returned at six. At weekends we saw him in the shops making his purchases without interest, and walking along the beach by himself. When it rained he sat with his back to the window. Clearly he had been desensitized.

I walked over to the Old Rectory by the cliff road. The downs were closed. *Keep Out*, the notice said.

'How's the tortoise?' I asked Fion.

'He's got a wife,' he said. 'They've moved to the garden. We can't go on the downs any more. Mutley is upset about it.'

'Julian asked for a sabbatical,' Olwen said, 'and they've given it. That's a blessing, although he'll be bound to worry about his pupils, though most of them have drifted off.'

'Olwen's still playing it down,' Julian said as he came into the room. 'You've heard the latest news?'

'Not today,' I said.

'We've been re-classified. We're no longer a safe area.' He picked up the chess board. 'Want a game?'

'Were we ever really safe?' I asked.

'Within bounds.' Julian set up the pieces.

I made a decision. 'I'm going to look at the downs,' I said.

'Don't be mad,' Olwen snapped.

'Why not?' Julian pushed the chess pieces off the board. 'The entrance through the copse is still unsignposted. We can always say we strayed—if questioned.'

'You are not to go,' Olwen screamed.

'We must,' Julian said. 'We must use all the facilities, even the limitations.'

'You needn't come with me,' I said.

'Oh, he must.' Olwen was sharp. 'He has to confront the possibilities.'

With the exhilaration of rashness we walked into the small copse behind the Old Rectory. The trees burgeoned with bud although spring was some weeks away. We reached the kissing-gate that led out to the downs. 'Let's kiss for luck,' I said. We climbed the first hill and stood at the top of the ridge. We could see all over the downs. To our left the sea. Larks soared and dived above our heads. There was no one in sight. We laughed with relief, joined hands, and ran down the slope. 'I wish I'd brought my dog.' I had left him in Fion's care. The sun shone fitfully, colouring first one area, then another. We walked for miles, up and down, down and up, breathing in the expanse of the empty landscape.

'We might be the only people left on earth,' I said.

'Come on.' Julian's voice was full of the gladness of relief. 'Up the hill again and then home, home for tea.'

We turned round. There they were on the ridge. We looked behind us. A similar column in line, each one holding a pole to match his height. They began to move, downwards, with deliberate precision. 'Hold my hand,' Julian said. 'We must go on, as we intended, homewards.'

They broke formation, in slow motion, gyrated towards us, executing a pattern of zigzagging movements, crossing and recrossing one another's steps.

'If we're lucky we'll miss the symmetry of their course,' Julian said.

We felt them as rank after rank of them moved past us. Pockets of air hit us as their intricate patterns of movement slid past us. I stumbled. Julian pulled me up fiercely. 'We mustn't alter our pace or sway in the slightest,' he said.

As we moved up the track they surrounded us on all sides, never deviating an inch from their rigid exercise. Others followed in their tracks. The crossings and recrossings of their lines went on, relentlessly slow, totally in unison. I was sweating. I was tired. I wanted to pause. Julian urged me upwards. I could see the kissing-gate in the distance. Another relay began their descent. 'Don't look back,' Julian said. 'Keep with the stream of our natural route.' I saw one of the poles as one of the men moved a fraction past my body: it shone like steel. To the left and the right of my vision they swirled. I pressed my arms closer to my body, fearing I might knock against one of the poles. Their precision was monstrously accurate as they repeated the motions of those who had descended before them. I caught glimpses of eyes, heads, chests, arms, legs, and, ever, the shining steel poles. I saw the last three of them as they veered towards us. One went to the right of us, the other to the left. Quickly Julian pushed me away from him as the third one crashed into the space between our two bodies, and went on.

We reached the kissing-gate. 'Don't look back,' Julian said. 'We must not appear inquisitive.' He sounded frivolous.

I stood on the other side of the gate and shook with fear delayed. 'Gambler's luck!' My hilarity was hysteria. 'A fraction here, a fraction there, we might have been trapped.' It came to me suddenly. 'That's how the old man died. Immobilized by fear.'

'Indeed!' Julian lit me a cigarette. 'At any time, any-where, in life.'

'And the dead dog outside my gate?'

'A warning,' Julian said. 'Or, shall we say in chess par-lance, a check.'

'Not a mate though—we've just come through,' I boasted.

'So far,' Julian said. 'Come on, let's go home for tea.'

THE FINE VALLEY

We stood quite still. Everything hummed with summer. We had turned off at the Victorian viaduct, into the woods, mounting slowly, until a decline brought us in sight of the valley. Acres of wheat glowed amber in the August afternoon. The luxuriousness of the enclosed fields was unexpected. I walked in front, Rick followed, my dog at the rear. The path was narrow, made more so by the proliferation of entangled bramble, wild flowers and berries bordering the wood on our side. We had crossed the field from the wood now facing us. There had been a moment of fear. The man on the canvas stool, a black retriever at his feet, gun pointed towards a clearing. Three shots expressed his indifference. 'Clay pigeons,' Rick said. We gave him a greeting which he ignored. It was a relief to come into the valley of wheat. Gunshots, faint yet decisive, told us that he was still there. The height of the wheat reached our waists.

'I'm glad country walks are still possible.' I leant against Rick, better to stress his participation in this summer splendour.

'They accept it as an extension to our activity, at least tacitly,' he said.

'Couldn't the villagers do the same?'

'Not easily. Figuratively they must show a reason. We're allowed breathing space, officially permitted periods of contemplation, within bounds of course.' Rick looked immortally youthful, sunlit against the background of wheat.

'Don't you meet anyone on your walks?'

'The odd forester, hedger, agricultural worker, and,' ironically, 'men with guns, like our friend over there.' Rick nodded towards the dark boundaries.

'I'm glad we came here straight away.' I breathed in scent of wheat and hedgerow, absorbing sound of insect, bird and small field rodents.

'After your journey I thought it would relax you.' Rick held the piece of crystal found in the wood to his eyes. 'This looks like a chip of meteorite. I'll get Adrian to analyse it—he's our amateur crystallographer.'

As though rising out of the wheat, cycling towards us, Adrian, Jill, the two boys, Dana in the lead, greeted us with joy.

'You're having tea with me,' Dana said as she wheeled past us.

As they swirled round the bend, they looked back and waved. We watched them out of sight.

We moved dreamily, sun-soaked, down through the valley of wheat. Where the stile met the road we saw the black retriever, crouching. I made to pat him. He slunk off. In the village we went past the neat houses with their closed windows and trim front gardens. There was no one in sight. We turned into the lane leading to the Norman church. An old woman was kneeling on one of the graves. She gave us the sign against the evil eye.

'Shouldn't we reassure her?' I asked.

Rick shook his head.

We found Ross in the studio pouring white acid over a glass panel. 'Tricky stage this,' he said as he went on working. Sun from the windows highlighted the reds, blues and yellows of his design. Rick opened the firing kiln and pulled out one of his trays. 'Well taken,' he said, as he closed the kiln door again and switched off the current.

I let myself out through one of the long windows and wandered about the park surrounding the house. Two oak trees, giants in circumference, were welded together, a natural union, spanning years of tune. Back against their trunk, I looked at the house, an eighteenth-century dignity, once an abode of privilege, now a communal Centre for those who still practised their art—painters, sculptors, potters, weavers. On the step of the loggia Dana sat. I ran towards her. 'Time for tea,' she said, giving me her hand.

On the way to her place I put my question. 'Has nothing been. . . ?'

'Intimated?' She finished my question. 'Not precisely. We lock our studios more carefully at night. I'm glad you came,' she said.

Tea was a return to childhood with home-made scones, dishes of jam, plates of bread and butter, watercress, boiled eggs, seed- and ginger-cakes. The boys were given fruit jellies.

'We'll have to be a little more cautious,' Adrian said when the boys went out to play. 'They've boarded up the post office. Redundant, they say. We are the only people who write and receive letters.'

'The villagers? Surely they must use it?' I asked.

'They've altogether lost the habit.' Adrian lit his pipe. 'Communication is not encouraged.'

Walking back to the house with Rick I said, 'I suppose that's the crux of the matter. Communication, I mean.'

'It's to be discouraged. That's why we carry on.' Rick gave me his hand.

We passed the neat houses with their closed windows and trim front gardens. I caught glimpses of television screens glowing faintly within. Rick followed my glance. 'They offered us all sets. Adrian accepted one, for the boys, and for news, such as it is.'

Rick led me to the grave where we had earlier seen the old woman. He bent down and traced out the poor lettering, reading the name and the dead man's occupation. *Glazier*, it read. 'He was her only son. He had ideas beyond his ordinary craft. That's why the old lady resents us. We represent a dangerous aspiration. He killed himself.'

'Why?' My voice was faint.

'They isolated him. The Centre wasn't here then. There was no refuge for him.' Rick pulled up a few weeds from the miserably tended grave.

Rick's living quarters, which he shared with Ross, were at the front of the house, on ground level. During the night I heard the feet, walking, running, scurrying to and fro. A few yelps, then silence. Ross went out. When he returned he said, 'Only some more broken fence in the grounds. No point repairing it.' He sounded bored.

Rick made some tea and sat on my bed talking about times of shared joy. I remembered my journey. The trip from the coast to London. Few private cars on the roads. Mostly lorries, public transport, military trucks: I caught whiffs of their compulsory radio programmes. The tedious delay in the investigation centre, computers rapping out their data. Credentials cleared, I drove northwards. I suppressed the urge to turn off the motorway to revisit villages and towns not on my destination route, knowing that radar checkpoints would refuse me entry. Passing through industrial cities I sweated, oppressed by the closed windows of tower block apartments. I had planned my journey not to coincide with the shopping hours of places through which I drove. I could not endure the 90 dB intensity of pop music that street megaphones relayed at such times.

'Open the window, Rick,' I said, needing the freedom.

'They watch our lights,' he said. 'We exceed the permitted time quota. We only survive here because of an obsolete law giving such centres as this ill-defined privileges. It'll be changed—in time!'

'Meanwhile?'

'Meanwile we carry on. Their tactics are soundly based—on the communal resentment we provoke.'

'Jealousy, you mean?' I asked.

'No, fear. We represent danger. Non-conformity is an illness. We're possible sources of contagion. We're offered opportunities to,' he gave a slight chuckle, 'integrate. Refusal is recorded as hostility.'

'And your work?'

'It remains in our studios. Our supply coupons are proportionally reduced. Food-wise we're substantially self-supporting.'

'Can you go on like this?' I cried out.

'One can go to the edge.' Rick switched off the light. 'Sleep well,' he said. 'We must use our time as creatively as possible, in talk, in work, in love. Communication lines must be preserved, kept open for others to use when they need them.'

'I will take some of your work back with me,' I said, 'to share with others on the coast.'

'You're boasting,' Rick said. 'No rashness. First explore the limitations.'

I woke early to another splendid summer day. Ross was already working.

'We've been offered a house,' Adrian said as we met in the grounds.

'Oh, no!' Fear touched me.

'It's the second time in four months.' Adrian grinned.

'I never acknowledge official forms. You may say I'm absent-minded.'

Rick and Dana were laughing at a shared joke when I joined them.

'You don't feel the strain?' My question was partly rhetorical.

'Less than you do, love, on the coast,' Rick said. 'We have each other. That's why we asked you to come, to break down some of the strain, so that you can return renewed.'

I thought of my coastguard's cottage where I worked, walked, shopped and talked to my dog. Neighbours, such as I had, kept their windows closed and their television sets on. I had refused the offer of a set. Equally perverse, I tended my small garden, not so trim as those of my neighbours, which the machines dealt with. I grew flowers and fruit. Periodically I left both flowers and fruit near my gate at night, gifts to those brave enough to accept them. Occasionally I put out a book but none dared take it. It was a way of talking.

'We do the same,' Dana said. 'Last week I had a triumph. I put one of my paintings out. It was taken.'

'How do you know it wasn't them?' I asked.

'They wouldn't want one ever to think that acceptance was possible,' Rick said.

'It may be worse with others.' I considered the matter. 'Others help one's courage, make one defiant.'

'Yet more secure, replenished as we are in our daily exchanges of love and talk. We act as safety valves for one another,' Rick said.

'Let's have a picnic, a pretend day,' Dana said.

'In the valley?' I asked.

We chose a small clearing just outside the wood overlooking the whole valley of wheat fields. We laughed, talked, played silly games, ate our picnic fare and, intermittently, dozed in the afternoon heat. I watched Dana make a necklace of wild flowers which she hung on my dog's neck. 'I'll paint you tomorrow,' she said. It was a token. I closed my eyes to stop the tears.

'I'm just going to explore a bit.' Rick wandered off into the wood. We watched his tall thin body move out of sight.

'Not to worry, love,' Dana said. 'He'll keep safe.' She took up one of her sketch-pads.

About an hour later Rick returned.

'They're building some more houses at the top of the wood,' he said. 'Nineteen, actually.'

There were nineteen of them at the Centre, counting each family unit as one, and Ross and Rick as two.

'But they can't, it's not legal . . .' I stammered.

'They're drafting a new bill at the moment. A matter of routine, of time,' said Rick.

'We'll join you on the coast,' Dana said. 'There are ways of getting through.'

'Be my guests.' I was merry with hysteria.

'Guests are suspect. We'll be your family,' Rick said.

'They've passed the new bill in the council,' Adrian said when we got back. 'Gradual abatement of the Art Centres. Operative from midnight. I think this calls for a party.'

We held the party in the lecture hall. No one spoke about the news repeated again on Adrian's television set. At midnight we went out, opening all the windows in the house. Then the lights flashed off.

'A power cut, most appropriately timed,' Ross said. 'Who's for candles?'

Those with wives and children were the first to be moved into the new houses. It was useless to protest if there were children to be considered.

'You will have to return to the coast now,' Rick said. 'We'll try and reach you later.'

Hypnotically I returned to the wheat fields. Ross accompanied me.

'They're getting ready for the harvest,' he said. 'Look in the hollow, the reaping machines are already there.'

Several studios were boarded up. Work left behind by those who had already moved into the houses was taken away. The house had a hollow sound; one was conscious of emptiness. Ross crated his work. Dana took her canvases into her living quarters. Rick arranged his in his studio as though preparing for an exhibition. I selected one of Rick's glass sculptures and placed it in my car. 'I'll risk it,' I said, when Rick advised against.

'They can't make you move?'

'From here? Yes,' said Rick. 'It's a legal closure of the Centre and its living quarters. They'll offer each of us a house, which we can refuse. It's all very correct in procedure, at this stage. There's the ambiguity of choice.'

'Like mine on the coast?' I recalled insisting on staying in the house I owned. Being already accommodated gave me a certain freedom, although the pressures to make my home like the neighbouring ones were many.

'Why did the others go? Adrian and Jill?' I asked.

'The children,' Rick said. 'Under age they must go, with or without parents. We shall have to find new accommodation, acceptable, within reason, to them. Difficult, yet not impossible. You were lucky to have your place before they launched their new housing scheme.'

'They might change those laws too.'

'Probably, in time, should they find they offer too great a threat.' He paused. 'You'd best stop the gifts at the gate for a while.'

'It's a way of keeping in touch,' I said.

'We'll keep in touch. Be sure of that.' Rick put his arm round my shoulders.

'I've another day left.' I smiled at him.

'Remember, visits are still officially allowed, occasionally that is, from one area to another.'

'Then why don't the others?'

'Avail themselves? They lose the touch—of keeping in touch. That's an art in itself. If one does it regularly it's noted as part of one's,' he grinned a little, 'lifestyle. In any case that anomaly may well legally be dealt with. They are continually adding clauses to new bills. The closure of post offices indicates the possibility. Do you know,' he said, 'I dream about telephoning.'

The next day Rick and I repeated our walk of the day of my arrival. Half the field was harvested. Returning we saw Dana cycling towards us. It had a *déjà vu* about it, except that Adrian, Jill and the two boys were not following in her tracks. There was no laughter in her face.

'Ross,' she cried. 'He made a stand. Claimed his crates as his property.'

'Oh God!' Rick said.

'They took him away,' Dana said.

'Listen!' Rick held us silent. We heard the second gunshot.

'Why?' I asked, although I knew.

'Intractability is a punishable offence. We'll bury him next to the other glazier,' Rick said.

As we walked down towards the stile the reaping machines moved further up the field. The black retriever raced across our path, snapping at my dog. Rick pushed Dana's bicycle. Dana and I joined hands as we followed him.

The house was all boarded up.

'I wish I'd put one of your paintings as well in my car,' I said to Dana.

'I can begin again, on your coast,' she said. 'We'll join you, somehow.'

The others had left. Dana picked some flowers and placed them in my car. Rick brought fruit. 'For your journey home,' he said.

'Will you really come?' I asked.

'We'll get through, love, we'll get through,' Rick said.

'Ross?' I hesitated.

'They'll bring him back here tomorrow. I'll bury him then.' Rick handed me the piece of crystal we had found in the wood on that first day of my visit. 'It's a bit of meteorite. Adrian was certain. You keep it. It's known so much space and time.'

I stroked the crystal. 'Souvenir of the fine valley,' I said.

I held Dana in my arms. 'Ciao, love,' I said.

I drove slowly away, past the neat houses with their closed windows and trim front gardens, on my journey back to the coast.

A LIGHT-HEARTED DAY

The day was light-hearted. A wind, slight and soft on the skin, enhanced rather than reduced the sun's warmth. Plumes of foaming waves surfaced like fresh paint on the sea. A day for falling in love. I took off my tennis shoes, rolled my slacks to the knee, paddled at the water's edge. I picked up my dog, threw him into the waves and watched him swim back to shore. A day for falling in love. The memory was a spur to imagination. Long time past such freedoms of will were possible. A time to smile and sing in the mornings. An ease of pace in living. I splashed handfuls of sea onto my face and licked the salt. A feeling of sexual need. I scooped about in the sand under the water and fished out a womb-shaped shell. A token for this light-hearted day. It would serve as a symbol to balance against the months of pain.

'Hallo there,' a voice shouted in my direction.

Sebastian ran down the slope to greet me.

'I've just come in,' he said.

He kicked off his sandals and joined me. We walked along the foreshore, slapping at the waves as they splashed inwards, imprinted our footsteps in the sand. Nearing the rocks we jumped from boulder to boulder, competing, like children, in speed. I slipped and fell into one of the rock-pools. Blood, brightly red, ran down my leg. Sebastian offered his handkerchief. Unhurt, I refused it, washing the cut with greenish water from the pool. The astringency was refreshing.

'Not to worry,' I said. 'We're all wounded.'

Sebastian insisted on binding the cut.

'It's good to know one can bleed,' I said. 'Almost exhilarating.'

Sebastian hugged me to him. 'It's a day for feeling again,' he said.

We put on our shoes and ambled over the sands.

'I asked Fiona to marry me yesterday,' he said. 'She wouldn't leave the retreat.'

'Oh dear!' I touched his arm.

'Not to worry,' he laughed. 'We're all wounded.'

'Why?' I asked.

'Fear, perhaps.' Sebastian sat down. 'They instil fear in the retreats. Fear of the world outside. No harm can reach one in a retreat. Quick acclimatization to loss of identity guaranteed.'

'And identity holds danger?' I knew it did.

'Wide open to it. Constantly vulnerable. The retreats offer peace—or should one say a vacuum of invulnerability.' He threw a pebble out to sea. 'I'm not giving up yet,' he said.

'Nor I.' I pulled him up from the sand. 'Come on, let's be defiant. There's a retreat a mile from here. Shall we pay a visit? They welcome trippers, so I'm told. There's always the possibility that some might stay.' I laughed at my imaginative flight of fancy.

'I've been fantasy-weaving too,' Sebastian said. 'I can't reach her. My letters remain unanswered. Yet every day I do ask her to marry me—in my mind.' He swirled round and shouted at the sea: 'Fiona, will you marry me? Fiona, marry me, please.'

I joined in the fantasy. 'Fiona,' I shouted at the sea. 'Please marry Sebastian. He will build you a house of colour facing a harbour of content.'

Sebastian's euphoria fell from him. 'Do you know what my next job is? Now, on my drawing-board?' He was an architect. 'A retreat. I told them I needed some leave. That's why I'm here—on holiday.'

'Can you refuse?'

'No. Actually, it's a challenge. No windows permitted. I shall have to create light through some other means. It must be possible.' He scooped up a handful of sand. 'Some substance like this, perhaps.'

Approaching us, half-running, five children, one girl and four boys. They jabbered like savages, indecipherable gang vocabulary. They eyed us with contempt. One of them held a milk bottle, waving it high like a trophy. One finger acted as a stopper. Sebastian grabbed it. It was partly filled with butterflies. He held it high. Slowly, some of the butterflies crawled up the bottle and flew out. The others were dead. Sebastian threw the bottle into the sea. Two of the boys kicked his ankles. I hit them as hard as I could. They ran off screaming abuse back at us. The girl stood her ground. I began to explain the cruelty and offence to nature's enriching bounty. 'You sloppy shit,' she said, and walked away.

We made our way back to my cottage in silence.

As we sat in the garden having lunch, something furry was flung over the gate. We heard jeers and feet running away. My dog pounced. I caught him, and pulled the mangled creature from his jaws. It was a kitten: both eyes had been gouged out. Sebastian took it from me and walked to the dustbin. I pushed my food away from me.

'They kept their eyes on us,' Sebastian said. 'We'd better keep ours on that creature there,' he nodded towards my dog. 'At least for a day or so, until they find some other target for their senseless violence.'

'Children will be children,' a voice said. It was my next-door neighbour. She had witnessed the incident.

'Quite!' Sebastian said.

'Your roses are giant blooms this year,' she said.

I offered to cut some for her.

'Just one,' she simpered.

I clipped off one of the larger blooms and gave it to her. She sniffed at it. Smiling at me, she placed her hand over the bloom, crushed the petals into a pulp, and dropped the stem at my feet. 'Thank you,' she said, and went indoors.

Sebastian was behind me. 'This is our light-hearted day, remember? Let's walk to the estuary, over the hills and through the woods.' He pocketed some hard-boiled eggs and apples. 'Grub for later. You'll eat then. Hunger always returns.'

I caught his mood, and picked up a packet of bitter chocolate.

A man followed us halfway up the first hill, thought better of it, and went back. At the top we sat down and looked up at the sky. A faint breeze dried our sweat. The grass was high enough to hide us from immediate sighting.

'Sebastian,' I said, 'yesterday my new manuscript was returned to me—by the post office. Torn into pieces. Damaged in transit, they said.'

'They take it upon themselves,' Sebastian said.

'Luke took a second copy up to town today,' I said.

Sebastian brought out the eggs from his pocket. I gave my dog a third of mine. A helicopter flew overhead.

'The isolation is getting worse,' I said. 'Why did Fiona go to the retreat?'

'Taken there,' Sebastian said. 'She could no longer sing. She became inactive. Certifiably so, by their standards. Opera is a dangerous art; it suggests too many freedoms.'

Above our heads birds swarmed, jubilant in their song.

'They keep her sedated,' Sebastian added. 'There are no doors inside a retreat. One is allowed to walk through all the rooms and corridors. No windows, of course. Air is filtered through a common vent. You might call it the meeting-place. Everyone congregates there. They look up at the vent expecting to see some sky. Nothing. Only a steel grill with pin-points through which some air flows. The only light comes from the television screens, kept on all the time. I'm told they don't notice the noise or the images after a while. At first it breaks them down. There's a television set in every room. I know from the blueprints they handed me yesterday for my new job. I'm to improve on older models. There have been lapses.'

'Lapses?' I asked.

'Some still feel pain. Are still vulnerable. This is put down to inefficient design. I am expected to correct the flaws.'

'And when all pain and feeling is drawn out?'

'They let them out. Cured—of identity.' Sebastian crushed his eggshell and scattered the powder over the grass.

We walked towards the woods. The track at the edge was cool and warm and full of soft, swift sounds: birds intently active, the odd squirrel scurried up a tree's bark, a rustle among the fern indicated small animals disturbed. Soon we would, through the clearing at the end of the track in the wood, glimpse the estuary in the distance. The grass beneath our feet felt like an untrodden lane of moss.

'Days like these,' I began.

'Are light-hearted,' chanted Sebastian.

'We could wish all miracles,' I said.

'And do high deeds.' Sebastian gave me his hand. Suddenly, he pulled me to a stop. In front of us a young man ran, panting. He crashed into the bracken. Following him, more steadily, four men. Each man carried a thick coil of rope. They did not glance at us as they passed. My dog barked at them and ran after them. Sebastian whistled him back. We walked on, increasing our speed. As we came to the clearing, within sight of the estuary, we heard the screams. Then silence.

The sea was a flat, shining extension of the sands. The landscape before us looked uninhabited, untouched, an unframed painting of a limitless horizon. At the bottom of the track was an old farmhouse.

'I need a drink of water,' I said to Sebastian.

'We'll ask,' he said.

The child at the door looked apprehensively at us.

'You can have a cup of tea,' the young woman said at Sebastian's request. 'I've just made a pot.'

We sat in the gloomy kitchen, glad of the cool.

'Come from the woods, have you?' asked the woman. We nodded.

'That was my husband.' Her voice was bleak. 'He refused to farm the new way. He loved his animals.' She pushed the child from her. 'I told him it would mean trouble.'

We finished our tea. Sebastian thanked her. At the door she clutched his arm. 'Will they take him to one of the retreats?' she asked. The child began to cry. The woman went inside and slammed the door behind her. We walked on, towards the estuary.

Moored to one of the banks was a gaily painted barge. Three young men and two girls hailed us. 'We're travellers,' they said. 'Come and join us.' They gave us cold drinks and fruit. They were non-residents, able to move where they chose, experts at avoiding trouble, scenting danger spots, working at odd tasks on their chartless way, picking up enough money for food and fuel for their boat. Never staying in one place, they provoked only transient distaste. Like gamblers they played their luck from day to day. They offered us hospitality and temporary friendliness. They were news-gatherers, being observant of much seen on their rootless chuffing up and down the canals. Joining them one had a false sense of security. They invited us to travel with them.

Sebastian placed our viewpoint before them: 'We both have work to do—our choice.'

They laughed the word away.

'We have freedom,' said one of the girls.

'For what?' Sebastian asked.

'For moving on,' one of the young men said.

We did not push the issue further. We each had danger in our prospect. We moved back into the light-hearted area of their afternoon conviviality. They were known as the harlequins, part zanies, part tricksters. Sometimes they were beaten up when they moored for the night by local polichinelles out for some quick fun. Weather permitting they would anchor their barge a little way away from the bank: experience taught them some caution.

We watched them as they chugged off back up the canal again, waved them out of sight.

'Perhaps we should do the same—just drift,' I said.

'Not in our stars.' Sebastian smiled. 'We have work to do.'

'For how long?' I asked.

'For ever and ever and ever.' He laughed. 'Forever vulnerable, in our light-hearted way.'

'And the pressures? The increasing isolations? The sharp loneliness?' I hammered my points.

'To be assimilated, used, communicated,' Sebastian said. 'There'll always be someone to listen, to see, to hear.'

'Keeping in touch?' I felt slightly defeated.

'Keeping the way open for creative imagination. There's always someone, somewhere, ready to receive whatever one can give. It's going to be a wonderful sunset,' he said.

The sun blazed like a red peony hung over the sky. We walked back along the beach. The tide was out. We repeated our morning dance over the rocks, jumping from one boulder to another. Gulls alternately whirled around and settled in rows on the breakwaters. We breathed in deep gulps of sea ozone. Our bodies tingled with the beautiful day. There had been moments of peril, near unbearable, yet, with gambler's luck, we had come through. I expressed all this by way of a thanksgiving to Sebastian.

'Relatively, love, you might say we have been light-hearted.' Sebastian flung a piece of driftwood through the air for my dog to catch.

Luke was standing at my gate. A sign, surely, that my manuscript had been safely delivered. He did not smile as we came up to him.

'Sebastian,' he said, 'Fiona is inside the house. She was released this morning.' He paused, unwilling to bring out the word. 'Cured,' he said.

We went indoors.

Fiona was sitting in a chair, head facing the window. Luke put a hand on my arm to stop me rushing forward. My dog barked and jumped trying to reach her lap. She took no notice of him. She turned her face towards us. There was no flicker of recognition. Our presence made no impact on her. She was totally unrelated. In no way vulnerable, in no way able to identify. She was, as Luke said, cured.

The pain was intense. We stood looking at Fiona, sharing the pain she would never again have knowledge of.

Sebastian moved towards her.

'Fiona,' he said. 'Fiona, will you marry me?'

THE FAIRING

Gusts of ground-mist spun rapidly towards and past me. High above the sun was a light lemon tone. A blue sky began to spread. My dog rolled on the damp grass. The morning held a fine promise. I had set out early. Not too early to attract any attention. I would follow the line of the cliffs until I came within sight of the lighthouse. The sea was a soft slow-motion expanse; waves seen from the cliff-top were minute curls of white foam. No boats in sight. To my left acres of downland topped here and there with small copses. I looked back. A haze of smoke rose from the hollow I had left behind. They were burning the stubble.

I stood still and looked down at the sea; the tide was on the turn. Gulls flew inland towards the cliffs, and, within inches of the chalk, swerved seawards again. The ground-mist evaporated. The sun gave out its heat. Down below on the shingle facing the sea were three men. One of them looked up. I drew back from the cliff edge. As I came to the bend in the range I saw the lighthouse in the distance. The landscape was softer; cliffs replaced by sloping shrubland and small trees. I followed the zigzagging path downwards through the tamarisks. At a turn in the track two middle-aged women came towards me. Carefully, I modulated my pace to one of quiet strolling. I did not wish to worry them; they had not noticed me coming towards them. I smiled at them as they drew nearer, and sensed their relief as I gave them a good-morning. At the bottom of the track I sat down to eat my bread and cheese.

'Take your time coming,' Tom had written. 'At every stage of the route be the casual stroller out for a short walk.'

I covered quite a few miles, rounded the coastline, and came onto the beach. Ahead of me was the village. The tide was full out. I walked over the wet sand. A little way out the lighthouse was sited, a more or less obsolete landmark. No more than a look-out post. A man was fishing from the crumbling landing-stage. I took off my sweater and tied it loosely round my shoulders. As I padded over the sands I kept a watch inland. I went to the edge of the sea, took off my tennis shoes, rolled my slacks to the knee, and paddled. As I stood looking at the sea fanning out before me I felt a quickening of pure physical exhilaration. I had forgotten that the world was round. Geometrically precise, the sea's curve on the horizon stressed a childhood wonder. Sea and sky offered a comfort. I rubbed sea water over my face and arms and swung round with sudden joy.

Running towards me were three swimmers. I held my breath as they rushed past me and flung themselves into the sea. For one moment I felt almost knocked over by their momentum. I had not noticed them before. I walked on, dribbling now and then at the small waves on the foreshore. Climbing over a breakwater I leant against the mussel-coated wall, put on my optical sun spectacles and

studied the beach before me. My dog barked. A black labrador lumbered towards us, wagging friendliness. A whistle
called him back to his owner, a tall thin man who nodded
as he skirted round me. I stroked the shell-encrusted breakwater, dug my fingers into clusters of seaweed, inhaled the
primeval scent of the consuming sea. There was no one in
sight. I set off again at a leisurely pace, willing myself to
be a physiological addition to sea and beach. Identification
with the landscape gave an illusion of invisibility.

I stumbled over a child scrabbling for crabs in a rock
pool. He hauled up a small creature, waved it in my face
and chortled. I made to tip his bucketful back into the
pool, stopped myself, and walked on. I had not noticed
him before.

'Move lightly,' Tom had written, 'as though you belong.'

As I neared the village I could see people stretched out
on the sands. On the small promenade some sat in deck
chairs. None strayed beyond the periphery of the desig-
nated beach. I came up to it by way of the sands. I might
have been there for some time. Many slumped, face downwards on their arms. I leashed my dog as I came into the
narrow high street, making for the bow-fronted tea-shop.
There was an empty seat in the window recess. I ordered
a cream tea. At the next table an elderly woman was crying. No one took any notice. 'You've been here before,' the
waitress said. I nodded.

'After the village,' Tom had written, 'remember the
fairing game. One three five repeat. It's now left to you.'

I understood the guidelines. In the past Tom and I
invented the fairing game as we drove through unknown
country. A number was chosen. We tossed a coin for left

or right, then drove until we reached the next road which coincided with our first digit, left or right hand side as the coin directed, and so on, until we arrived at the last digit. A voyage of discovery. We never knew what we might expect at the end of our random sequence. Often we were lucky and reached a beautiful place. I named our game the fairing since, through chance, symbolized by the fair, we might arrive at a fair place.

'One day,' I had said to Tom, 'I'll find my own fairing in this way.'

Tom had found his, and I was going to its security. He devised this way to direct me to his place because it was not wise to name it in a letter which they might read.

Whatever happened after leaving the village I must not deviate from Tom's number sequence; any going back in my tracks, for whatever reason, would confuse the direction which, once altered, might be impossible to find again. Before making for the road out of the village, I walked round the green and fed the ducks in the pond with a bun left over from my tea. I stepped aside quickly as two boys rushed at me. I had not noticed them. I sat on the wooden bench under the tree branches overhanging from the house behind the walled garden. The scene was a familiar one. I knew every detail of its prospect; it contained much of my past life. I felt tempted to remain. Being neither resident nor, strictly speaking, visitor, I had to move on.

Two youths lounged against a signpost at the road leading out of the village. One started towards me. The other pulled him back. I went on, conscious that they were watching me. I sighed with relief as the road curved, thereby placing me out of their sight. After some eleven minutes I came to the first turning off on the left. Toll-houses on either side of the road suggested a happy channel into the fairing. The road was narrow and winding, trees on either side met overhead in a natural canopy. The incline was slightly uphill. On the right there was a clearing in the wood. A man on horseback up against a wooden gate. At first I did not notice him. He touched his cap. I nodded in return for his greeting. The going sloped more upwards. At another bend of the road, motionless, in front of another wooden gate leading to a clearing in the wood on that side, another man on horseback. I prepared myself to nod a greeting. He did not touch his cap. The horse snorted at my dog. Not looking back I heard the rider cross the road and trot down the way I had come.

The canopy of trees over the road thickened. I stood still and listened. Only the sound of wood-pigeons cooing to each other was audible. Comforted in some measure, I hurried along, anxious to reach a clearer stretch of road. Sudden panic: had I missed a turning? I had been so concentrated on covering ground that I had not, consciously, been looking. One was within sight. I dismissed my fears, and counted this turning as the first of the next three digits. A little further on I came up to the second left turning. A lodge occupied one corner. A woman was sitting in a hardback chair; she watched me go by. I looked back. She had gone into the lodge. A clearing ahead where the canopy of trees ceased. As I came into the sunlight again I saw that I was on top of a hill, and the road now curved downwards. I could see a river in the distance and, faintly, made out the position of the third turning on my left.

Lush meadowland on both sides of the road rid me of the claustrophobic haze I had endured under the spreading trees. I looked at my watch; it was nearing six in the evening. How much longer, I wondered? I swung downhill and found myself crossing a small bridge over the river. I stood on the bridge's hump and looked down. A young woman sat on the river bank dangling her legs in the water. She smiled up at me. A young man, whom I had not noticed, scrambled out of the river and grabbed the young woman by an arm. She made a gesture of protest. He hit her in the face. She bent her head towards her lap. He stood and stared up at me. I walked on, leaving the river behind.

Automatically I swung into the third turning on my left, trying to eradicate the nasty incident from my mind. I passed the next left road almost immediately, ticking it off in my mind as the first of Tom's final digit. A straggle of nondescript dwellings spaced a few yards apart suggested the outskirts of a hamlet. I was alert, conscious that new roads might follow. None did, nor was there any village. I was hot, tired and thirsty. At the next turning I saw a pub. I went inside and ordered a cider, taking it to drink on the seat in the porch. Three men, each in turn, came out and stood for a moment, looking at me, then returned inside. I left my glass on the seat. Footsteps behind me. I hurried on. Someone touched my arm. I turned round.

'Your dog's lead,' the man said, handing it to me.

I thanked him and sweated at my panic reaction.

At the next crossroad a Norman church. I pushed through the lych-gate and walked towards the porch. The door was unlatched. I went in. Stained-glass windows through which some of the evening sun filtered illuminated the nave. I stared at a mutilated Saint Sebastian, elongated and yellow, at his feet a black thin dog. A pillar of the south arch of the chancel bore a circle four inches across, probably a stonemason's mark. On the north wall of the nave a stone head, eyes closed, mouth open. I traced its features with my fingers. The floor was flagged. It was damp. I shuddered and turned towards the door. A woman wearing a hat was sitting in one of the pews. I picked up my dog, dropped some coins into the collection box, and went out. Two large upright stones I had not before noticed stood near the porch.

'The village stocks.' The woman in the church was behind me. 'Years ago, of course.'

'Of course,' I said.

She bumbled away. Looking after her I noticed the round flint tower attached to the church. I knew what it was, a watch-tower. Approaching invaders were sighted from such towers in the past. As I glanced upwards I thought I saw movement, a face, a body sliding out of sight. It could have been an owl limbering up for his nocturnal flight.

Past the church the fourth turning. The light was fading. I hoped the final turning would not be too far away. The road was dusty, narrow, almost a farm track, and alternatively veered to the left and the right in a series of bends. I lost my sense of direction. A wooden gate in front of me. I nearly missed the fifth turning left. Another farm track bordering a wood which curved round. I saw I was on a hill overlooking a wide prospect of meadows. I could see a river in the distance, probably the same one I had earlier passed. The track ended abruptly. There was no house in sight. I totally lost my bearings. Had I made a mistake in my calculations? Missed a turning somewhere on the way? I turned round and round searching for a clue. Something moved in the wood behind me. My dog barked. A sound of flight. It might have been a pheasant. I heard a gunshot. Had Tom miscalculated? A man with a gun stepped from a clearing a little way ahead of me. He glanced at me, then trudged off along the track I had come by. The silence was frightening. No sound of birds: they had nested for the night.

I could see the moon faintly outlined. Clusters of stars were beginning to reveal themselves. The night promised to be bright and clear. Looking back at the track along which I had come I noticed a turning on my left. In coming I had only concentrated on left-hand turnings, vaguely conscious that other turnings were on the right-hand side of the route. Then I remembered. Repeat, Tom had written, repeat one three five. I ran towards the turning, a lane between tall hedges, curving leftwards and downhill. At the bottom a crossroads. I followed my next left turn. The moon was coming into its full luminosity; it gave me the light I needed. Then I saw the church, the same Norman church. By way of a deviation I was coming back to my previous route. The next turning would lead me to the pub. There I would get some food and a drink. As I touched the old stock stones I saw the woman in the hat again, watching me from the porch. She came over to me.

'You are not welcome,' she said.

She wore large round spectacles. Her back was to the moon. I could not distinguish her features or her expression.

'Saint Sebastian will not protect you,' she added.

'His wounds were not mortal.' My response was instinctive.

She hissed at me and scurried into the church. I felt faint and steadied myself by hanging onto the ancient stock stones, arms stretched between the two upright slabs. Shaking my head clear of a temporary blurring of vision I lifted it high, towards the flint watch-tower. A man was looking down. I hurried away towards the pub. I tried to recall what turning I had noticed on the right-hand side of the road on my first trip. There was one more to follow in Tom's second digit. I could not remember any. This meant I would have to go up the hill, over the river bridge, past the lodge, and along the tree-covered road. I wondered whether I should abandon the whole thing and stay at the pub for the night, if that were possible.

'Going far?' It was the same man who earlier had brought me the dog's lead I had left on the seat outside. He was younger than I remembered.

'To the main road,' I said.

'I'll give you a lift,' he said.

I hesitated.

'It's a fair way,' he said.

I followed him outside.

He owned a small farm van; it smelt of straw and cow dung.

'They'll be busy tonight,' he said, 'looking for folk outside their area.' He asked no questions.

I was glad of his canvas top. It gave a feeling of protection. We drove over the river bridge. I could see several people on the towpath; they were flashing torches on and off.

'You could take a nap,' my driver said.

I eased myself down further in my seat. My driver slowed down. Without looking I knew we had reached the lodge.

'They know my van around here,' he said. I realized his reduction of speed was to aid instant identification. I caught a glimpse of the woman in the lodge peering into the van as we passed. My driver rubbed his windscreen with his left arm, thereby obscuring any sight of me. He picked up speed again as we came into the canopy of spreading trees. In his headlights I saw in the distance the two riders, one on either side of the road. The one on the right rode across to the other side. His horse whinnied. I shivered but said nothing. At the main road my driver stopped. I thanked him. He patted my dog.

I turned left. There remained five left turnings in Tom's final digit. A sharp turn off the main road immediately brought me to another left turning. Relieved that two were reached within such a short time I ran into the second turning. A steep hill led downwards. The way ahead looked extremely dark. I leashed my dog and moved forward cautiously. After some little time I heard footsteps. I stopped. The footsteps stopped. I went on. The sound of footsteps started up again. Clear hollow sounds. The light was dim. I looked up. I had not noticed I was walking through a tunnel. The footsteps I heard were echoes of my own. I sighed with relief and wiped the sweat from the back of my neck. Above my head an odd tapping, not quite footsteps, yet similar. I listened carefully. I was under another road, under the road with the spreading canopy of trees. The sound was of horses' hooves. Frightened almost beyond panic I moved slowly on. I could now see an opening ahead. I was coming out of the tunnel. Ahead, to the left, I saw another turning.

How exposed would I be when I emerged from the tunnel? The distance to the next turning was relatively short. I decided to creep forward slowly. In running I might slip, fall, make a noise, cause my dog to bark. Overhead I heard the trotting horses, to and fro, from left to right, crossing and recrossing each other's tracks. I could only pray that the riders met in the middle of their road as I came out of the tunnel. I picked up my dog. I moved forward as in a nightmare. I heard the horses behind me. Quickly I turned leftwards into a lane encapsulated between high hedges. I leant against the bramble and sighed with relief. I was out of sight.

The lane curved in a semicircle. I let my dog jump to the ground, yet kept him on the lead. Dimly, far ahead, I could see a reflection from house lights. Two youths ran towards me. My dog barked. They snarled at him in mock canine yowls. I tripped over an old milestone, cursed, rubbed my ankle, then saw the last turning. I ran towards it and along it. I stopped dead in my tracks, faced by a wall, a high wall, the end of the final digit.

I beat on the wall. I was furious, and frustrated. My dog barked, a series of excited yaps. I looked closer at the wall. I had not noticed there was a gate in the wall. A wooden gate, green with age. My hands searched for a latch, a knob, a keyhole: there was none. I pushed my weight against it: it was rocklike in its ancient substance. Either it was bolted from the other side or totally inoperative as a gate. The wall had a familiar look. Then I recognized it. It was the high wall surrounding the house on the village green. I had journeyed through several circles in order to return.

'Hallo,' said Tom as he opened the gate to me. 'You've made it. I thought you would.' He drew me into the garden bolted the gate behind us, and gave me his hand. 'They're waiting for you,' he said.

THE GARDEN

Egon ran to the crumbling wall.

'Careful,' I shouted.

He jumped onto the parapet. I closed my eyes. The drop behind him was perpendicular, a cliff range, devoid of ledges, descending straight to the beach. He jumped back onto the grass and hugged me. 'It's magnificent,' he said, staring back at the garden. 'I'll paint every inch of it.'

'Don't do that again,' I said. 'That wall's centuries old.'

'Like the garden?'

'Yes, I suppose it's always been here. Someone in the eighteenth century went to work on it, taming the trees, constructing the arbours, building the summer-house, creating the rose garden, landscaping, decorating a wilderness.'

'A pleasure garden?' Egon enthused. 'For exclusive pleasure?'

'Once it was,' I said. 'Now it's common ground. Periodically they cut the grass, prune a few shrubs, plant more bulbs, replace broken seats. What walls remain are crumbling. Storms have shaped the trees this end, bent the tops of their branches northwards. Salt from the sea takes its toll.'

'And what a view!' Egon turned round again and looked down at the sea.

All the splendour of high summer surrounded us. The sky a Prussian blue, the sea awash with sunlight, the beach a cinnamon stretch of sand. From where we stood the garden, high on the cliff, was an undulation of variegated green splashed here and there with the yellows, mauves, pinks of flowering shrubs. Clumps of rosemary and lavender grew like weeds. The profusion of scents intoxicated. The damp sharp smell of newly mown grass stirred areas of childhood memories. Egon turned a couple of somersaults and fell face downwards on the turf. A circular concentration of daisies made a halo to his head. I moved towards the rose garden. Egon ran after me. Together we went into the enclosure of tall yew hedges. Their height and thickness intensified the scent of the old-fashioned blooms. We sat on the stone seat. We were within a perfect circle.

'This is magical,' Egon said.

'Pure luxury,' I said.

The colour range of the roses created a luscious sensual profligacy. The heat, the scent, the colour relaxed every nerve in my body. No view of the sea from the enclosed rose-garden. Only the blue sky overhead isolated us in a kernel of voluptuousness.

'This on your doorstep.' Egon slanted his eyes towards the direction of my cottage.

'Come,' I said, 'I'll show you the tunnel.'

Outside the yew enclosure it felt almost chilly, so overheated was the blood after time spent in the rose-garden. I led Egon back to the central hub of the garden, a conclave of trees which concealed the incline and entrance to the tunnel. A massive excavation of brick, dark and damp, a gothic gradient declining to a high wrought-iron gate through which a landscape of sun glittered.

Egon called to the echo of his own voice as we half ran down towards the gate.

Three children rushed past us, whistling.

'Sometimes,' I said, 'they lock the gate.'

It was not locked now. The children pushed it open and we followed through. We were on the beach, facing the sea. We looked up at the cliff, a dazzle of white. We ran towards the waves. My dog dug frantically in the sand. The children howled past us, splashing into the sea.

'Christ!' said Egon as he went after them. He caught one of them. The children screamed at him. Egon swore at them. They ran off. He came back to me cradling a small wet creature. It was a fox cub.

'They were trying to drown it,' he said.

'Let's take it back to the garden,' I said. 'That's where they live.'

Egon attempted to dry the cub with his handkerchief. It bit him. We pushed the gate open and released it. The cub scurried away up through the tunnel. Blood was pouring from Egon's fist.

'Let's get back quickly,' I said, 'and disinfect that bite.'

We walked through the garden, past the summer-house and the rose-garden, to my cottage. From my gate I could see some of the garden trees and a portion of the wall.

'Just as well it's my left hand,' Egon said.

'In the garden it's easy to forget,' I said.

'I forget most of the time,' Egon said. 'I have so much work to do. I won't be stopped.'

After tea Egon drew sketch after sketch, working rapidly, at full pressure. They all related to the garden. He had taken over my outhouse, using it as his workroom. He had lost his studio in London. Gleaned, as they called it, an allegory taken from reaper's waste. To protest would have been useless. He left, taking what materials he could salvage from their demolition task. It had been an arbitrary event, a matter of chance. The studio next to Egon's had not been touched. One was enough to serve as a warning.

Later that evening we called at the boathouse. We sat on Mike's veranda, drinking Muscadet, looking out to sea. The heat of the day still hung in the air. We had met no one on our way there. People usually stayed indoors at night.

'Why did you give up?' Egon challenged Mike.

'I haven't,' Mike said. 'I'm just resting. Building boats is in my blood anyway. An old family business. I thought it would serve me while I waited.' He paused slightly. 'And watched.'

'I'll never give up,' Egon said.

Mike smiled. 'I'm using the time for replenishment. I'll be ready when it eases up.'

'Will it?' I asked.

'Not yet I think,' Mike said. He was a sculptor. After they had gleaned him from the east coast he had come south, back to his roots, and revived his father's craft. Being utilitarian, it was countenanced, although open to some scrutiny. Individual arts and crafts were not legally disallowed, rather discouraged. Teamwork was the official norm.

'I'll take my sketch-book to the garden tomorrow,' said Egon.

'Go slowly,' Mike said. 'They are taking a survey of this area. Once gleaned, you're on the list.'

They argued for about an hour. In a few days Thoby would arrive and teach Egon some caution.

'Let's go home through the garden.' Egon was obsessed by it.

We heard the vixen call to her cubs, an eerie sound. Someone was running down through the tunnel. The echoes of footsteps reached us. We heard the gate clang as it was pushed open, then shut. The moon picked out lanes of light. A faint breeze came from the sea. The fretwork of the summer-house looked like lace in the moonlight. We went in. A young woman was stretched out on the floor. She was moaning. A siren wailed. Two ambulance men appeared with a stretcher. We stood outside. The young woman was taken away. Another man whom we had not noticed approaching went in with a bucket. He scattered sawdust over the glutinous patches of blood, then left. There was nothing to say; one asked no questions.

We walked slowly to the cliff-edge wall. Out at sea, at the end of the jetty, a three-tiered square rig was moored. The lights inside cast reflections in ripples over the sea.

'What's that?' Egon asked.

'A survey rig,' I said. 'They move along the coast. Mike was right. It's our turn now.'

Dimly we could see men climbing up and down the ladders, moving from one stage to another, scurrying along platforms. We heard the ambulance in the distance.

About four in the morning I woke Egon to tell him my dream.

'I dreamt my death,' I said. 'I was strapped down onto a horse's back. A helmeted soldier holding a long spear tipped by a huge hammer beat down on my back. Three times. I heard the horse scream. The soldier was quite impersonal. We were on a loggia fronting a tall square tower. The sun was Mediterranean. I saw my eyes; they were blue. The pain was excruciating. I feel the burning still.'

Egon gently stroked my back. 'Christ!' he said. 'The bite's reopened.' He rubbed the blood from his hand off my skin.

I made some tea, and opened the windows. I could smell the sea, hear the waves. Dawn was already in the sky. Someone was coming through my garden gate. My dog barked.

'Hallo,' said Thoby, 'I got here as fast as I could. I thought you might need me.'

'I'm going to catch dawn in the garden.' Egon pulled on some jeans and a sweater, gathered up his sketch-book and pencils and went out.

'And we'll have breakfast in the open air—*à la belle étoile*!' Thoby's grin was reassuring. 'I've come from the island,' he said. 'Left my boat at Mike's.'

'Egon's reckless,' I said.

'That's why I came,' Thoby said. 'I thought he'd be here.'

'Can you . . . ?' I hesitated.

'Stop him? No, I wouldn't do that. I can only watch out for him. That destruction of his studio acts like an inspiration on him. One wouldn't stop that.'

'Not even if . . . ?'

'Would you want me to stop you?' Thoby held out his hand.

After breakfast and baths we went to the village. On the green we saw the laminated notice, *Survey in Progress.* The slight air of general unease did not disturb us. We recognized it as a natural reaction. Surveys were ambivalent. No one quite knew how they operated. Rumours conflicted. The personnel attached to a survey were random in behaviour. Sometimes they stayed on the rig, sometimes they came on shore. It was considered unwise to move outside one's own area when they were in the vicinity. Reports hinted at concealed long-range television equipment; there was some evidence of radio communications. It was best not to notice or rather to avoid any air of noticing. Best to carry on, normally. Some could not bear the strain and broke down, although none could define the extent of the scrutiny endured. Occasionally someone was gleaned, usually someone working alone, at some art or craft. An almost disinterested destruction of the work took place. Nothing more, unless the individual whose work it was made a stand.

'I've remembered,' I said, 'that young woman last night.' I explained the incident to Thoby. 'She was a weaver.' I remembered more. 'She was working on a series of patterns inspired by the garden.'

I hurried Thoby down a side street. We walked warily towards the barn which had served as a workshop. The windows were broken. We looked in. The loom was smashed. A black cat brushed against my legs. Thoby went inside, found it some food and milk. We went back to the main street and made our purchases.

I was not surprised by the influx of sightseers. Like locusts they migrated in the wake of a survey. They moved sluggishly about an area under surveillance, relieving their apathy with small acts of vandalism, chucking their litter about the streets, staring at all whom they met with malicious intent, pushing people out of their way. They encouraged their children to stone the domestic animals: often there were fatalities. At night they prowled under the windows, peered in where they could, yowled when they thought people were asleep, smashed milk-bottles, threw beer-cans and often urinated and defecated in doorways. Physically they presented a uniformity of ugliness, their movements suggested the grotesque. They were on the look-out: sightseers for a gleaning which a survey might always bring about. If nothing happened they became a shade more fractious, and let out their suppressed cruelty in mischievous violence—anything from destroying a garden to brutalizing a stray cat. If a gleaning took place they would swarm to the scene of destruction, titillated by every detail of the event, their faces puffy with relish. It was the only time one saw them smile. Afterwards they would depart as sluggishly as they had arrived.

We made for the garden. The sightseers did not go into the garden. Little groups of them straddled themselves out-side the crumbling walls. We found Egon. As we came back into the street Egon dropped his sketchbook. It fell open. I bent to pick it up. The sightseers surrounded me. Egon darted forward. 'It's mine,' he said defiantly. The sightseers muttered among themselves. Thoby stopped Egon speaking to them.

Mike was waiting for us when we got back. He stayed to lunch. Over coffee he said: 'Two of them came to my boathouse this morning. A small repair job on one of their skiffs. I saw to it that they took a good look round. I've taken on an extra hand, to suggest a thriving teamwork business.' He paused fractionally. 'They won't come back. I suggest, Egon, you transfer your work to my quarters, temporarily. We don't want this place to be a target, do we?'

'That's why I'm here,' Thoby said. 'To make a team.'

'I'm not afraid,' I said.

'You and I are working together on a book.' He grinned. 'I'll sit with a load of reference books in my lap while you work.'

'I'm not stopping, even temporarily,' Egon said.

'Of course not.' Thoby leafed through Egon's sketch-book. 'You've enough here for the paintings.'

'Not yet.' Egon stood up. 'I've reserved the yew enclosure for this afternoon.'

'Couldn't it wait?' I had to ask.

'No, love,' Egon said. 'If I wait I'll lose it.'

I watched him go. At the gate he blew us a kiss.

Mike and Thoby loaded Egon's gear from the outhouse into Mike's van.

I took my dog to the beach and sat looking at the sea for about an hour. The rig looked like a giant crane. It showed no sign of life. There were no sightseers on the beach. Only a few children splashing about in the water. I got up and went towards the garden tunnel gate. There, on either side of the gate, were two groups of sightseers lolling against the cliff. I nearly turned back. I leashed my dog and pushed open the gate. It slammed behind me. I looked back. The sightseers were peering in. They made no move to follow. I walked up the tunnel, deliberately casual in my pace. Coming out, through the trees, I felt the heat of the day and caught the garden scents. From where I stood I could see the garden's whole contour. I picked a sprig of rosemary and sniffed at the small blue flowers. Some indefinable sound made me look carefully about me. Outside the crumbling walls were the sightseers, in rows like sentinels, peering in. What I heard was a communal note of excited expectation.

'Egon,' I shouted, then stopped.

Circuitously I made my way to the yew enclosure. Egon was not there. Something on the grass caught my eye. I picked it up. It was a 5B black crayon. I sat down on the seat and sweated. The colours of the roses merged in my view of them. The sound outside was more audible. I realized that it was increasing. Then suddenly silence. Thoby ran in.

'Have you seen him?' he asked.

I showed him the 5B pencil.

'They came to your outhouse, found nothing, and went away,' Thoby said.

We went out of the yew enclosure. Thoby held my hand. The lines of watching sightseers had doubled.

'They have a nose for danger,' Thoby said, 'danger for someone else.'

'Why don't they come into the garden?' I asked.

'Distrust,' Thoby said. 'The garden is beauty, is sensuality, is mystery, is imagination. They sense a trap.'

'And we come here because of these?'

'Yes, it's our trap. The sightseers prefer concrete. Think of their passion for marinas, not for the boats, but for the car parks, the amusement arcades, the proliferation of restaurants and blocks of high-tower apartments. They like to see the sea pulverized out of its natural area by concrete. They dislike the beaches for the same reasons; bathing in the sea is too uneasy a freedom, they prefer swimming pools. They like nothing better than to sit in their cars and look at the sea from the safe harbour of a monstrous marina complex.'

'Our trap?' I held onto the word. 'Is that why the garden is left untouched?'

'In a way. We do walk into it, don't we? Drawn by its dangerous fantasy. Yes,' Thoby looked sad for a moment, 'we walk willingly into the trap.'

'As Egon has?' I asked.

Then we saw them, three of them, striding through the sightseers, coming into the garden. They went towards the summer-house.

The door of the summer-house opened. Egon, clutching his sketch-book, came out. He saw them. He stood quite still for a moment, then ran.

'Stop him,' I said.

Thoby ran after him but he was not quick enough. They surrounded Egon. He threw his sketch-book at them, and raced towards the wall bordering the cliff edge. He jumped onto the parapet. They came in closer to him. I picked up the sketch-book. Egon laughed. He fell backwards, arms splaying outwards. The three men turned and stalked towards the sightseers.

Momentarily paralysed, I saw the sightseers drift sluggishly away. Thoby ran towards the tunnel. I threw the 5B pencil on the grass and rushed after him.

Egon's body was pitched against the gate. Thoby, opening it, jolted the body; it rolled limply. Before Thoby could stop me I bent down. Thoby pulled me up. I stared at the blood on my hand.

'Go and fetch Mike,' Thoby said.

As I made my way back through the garden, past the summer-house and the rose enclosure and out into the village, I saw them dismantling the *Survey in Progress* sign. I was still carrying Egon's sketch-book; it was smudged with blood from my hand.

HALLO LOVE

'Hallo love,' I said, every day to each morning. A greeting to space and time. A ritual. Keeping my hand in. It was always possible that through space and in time it might be heard. I opened the windows and smelt the lushness of summer. I went out to the garden, checked what new blooms had flowered overnight, touched the oleander-like softness of the pink-petalled, melon-shaped hydrangeas, watered my collection of beach pebbles set out on the window-sills, alms to fortune. Impregnated, they glistened in a galaxy of subdued colour. I sat in the garden and let the sun's warmth draw sweat from my body.

I could see the sea, a beatitude of blue. When Tim came we would go swimming. My dog ran down the slope to the beach. He pounced on some driftwood and brought it to my gate. I went indoors, tidied the house, had my bath. Sun rays shone through the muiti-coloured glass panel Tim had made for me. I touched the surface, fingering each droplet; every shade of colour in the spectrum was incorporated. The house was ready to receive guests.

Tim brought a basket of plums. We took some with us to the beach.

'You don't lock up?' Tim looked back at the cottage.

'No point,' I said.

We played dolphins as we splashed in the waves. Tim swam far out to sea. I floated on my back. My dog barked at the water's edge. I could see the top half of the tower.

After we had dried ourselves in the sun and eaten the plums, we walked to the village, past the tower which had no windows. Two streets away the grey lodge, blinds pulled down, looked uninhabited.

'No news?' Tim asked.

I shook my head, pain rushing back to scald the memory.

In the village shop we bought eggs, bread and tomatoes. The couple who lived next door to me stood outside on the pavement, quarrelling. The shopkeeper grinned with pleasure. 'It's a form of communication,' Tim said.

'A stream of visitors at the grey lodge every night,' the shopkeeper hissed. 'All the lights on, full on.' Tim picked up his change. 'Spongers, flatterers.' The shopkeeper glared at Tim. 'Company of course,' she said. We went out.

'I wish it weren't so near,' I said to Tim.

'It would always be near no matter where it was.' Tim held my hand. 'One must accept the circles of envy and frustration. Isolate oneself from them. Let them burn themselves out.'

'They are self-renewing,' I said.

Indoors, instinctively I picked out the book from my shelf. 'Another inscription torn out.' I showed the book to Tim.

'It can't cancel the gift,' he said as he held me to him. 'The pressures are increasing.' He replaced the book.

I sat in the garden while Tim prepared lunch. I heard him singing in the kitchen. The shopkeeper's malice was exorcized as I realized that I was still alive, able, through space and time, to keep my hand in. 'Hallo love,' I said, as Tim appeared with a luncheon tray. 'I'm practising,' I added.

'Keep it up, it could be catching.' Tim served the food. 'We have a call to make this afternoon.'

I remembered. 'Won't it be noticed?'

'Do we mind?' Tim said.

After lunch we drove inland. We were twice stopped. Tim showed his traveller's pass. They waved us on. We wound down all the car windows. The heat was thickening. We turned off the motorway into the pitted lanes. Over the bridge, slowly, because of the deep ruts on the disused track. The Folly faced us. Tim got out and opened a ramshackle gate. Alarmed, dozens of guinea pigs scurried to safety on the bank of the muddy stream. We drove carefully into the courtyard.

It had once been a perfect model of an early nineteenth-century dairy. Now, its complex of stalls, barns, granaries was dilapidated, uncared for, a rubbish dump. The bell in the clock-tower was rusted. The dovecote taken over by indigenous pigeons. Tessa's residential quarters were equally neglected; a gipsyish encampment of rooms cluttered with toys, clothes, packing-cases, stores and dust-laden, ill-assorted furniture. A Blüthner stood alone in a whitewashed cell. Tessa's greeting was over-exuberant. The autistic child clung to her. The other boy took me on a tour of the Folly and initiated me into a series of fantasy games. He was fair and beautiful and impervious to the ruin about him, intent above all else to assert an independent happiness. 'Will you stay here with me?' he asked. We returned to Tessa and Tim.

'What will you have?' Tessa asked. 'I can give you anything you like. He left me well provided for. You can see that. We have everything we need. I'm going to get a tutor for the boys. There is nothing we lack. Look around, we're well stocked up. We are surrounded by plenty. I want to turn this place into a theatre, a theatre of the arts. We can all do our thing. We have always kept open house. Everything is ready. We lack nothing. I have lots of money.'

'We'll have some tea, Tessa, please,' Tim said. 'Shall I make it?' He set about the task.

Tessa sat down and wept. The autistic child kicked her. The other boy drew me out into the courtyard. 'She does nothing,' he said. 'I can jump higher than you. Watch me.' He leapt from the steps leading to one of the upper store-rooms.

I went back to the kitchen room.

'I won't leave,' Tessa was saying to Tim. 'This is my house. I bought it for him. I filled it with everything he could want. I won't go. He may come back.'

'Tessa,' Tim spoke gently, 'he's dead. He won't come back. You must go away, leave this ruin, begin again somewhere else, with the boys—for their sake, please.'

'This is mine,' she wailed. 'My life is all here.'

'You've let it disintegrate, Tessa.' Tim drew patterns for the austistic child.

'When he comes back he'll rebuild. He'll make the place beautiful. I'm looking after it for him, keeping it safe.'

'It isn't safe, Tessa, not here,' Tim said. 'You must get far away.'

'They can't make me go. This is mine—my life is here.'

'Your grief is here,' Tim said. 'You are in danger, so are the boys.'

'I will show you,' Tessa sprang up, 'I will show you every piece of my life.'

We followed her frenzied course through the Folly. The autistic child clung to her. The other boy winked at me and danced on ahead, intent on his own happiness. We landscaped the Folly that held Tessa's love. Passing the clock-tower I looked up at the sixty-foot iron ladder welded into one side of the inner wall. He had thought to hide under the huge bell when they came to take him away. A few rungs from the top he slipped. Tessa was the first to reach his body. He was a poet and wrote about the need for love. Tim picked up the autistic child and heaved him onto his back. The boy chanted with pleasure and jigged his heels into Tim's shoulders as though straddling a pony.

'Tessa, please,' I pleaded. 'Get away with the boys. Please.'

Her face was blank. She moved like a zombie from barn to granary, over the broken planks, kicking at the debris and decay of the past year, jerking into hectic speech, random memories of her lost love, beating her head against the rotten wood, clawing at the tangled thatch. 'It's mine, mine, mine,' she moaned.

'It's your distress,' I said.

'It's all I have left,' she said, then almost calmly, 'I'll not deny the pain.'

We saw them drive their covered jeep into the court-yard. Unresisting, Tessa let them lead her to the jeep. Tim rushed forward. 'We'll return for the boys later,' one of them said.

'I'm taking them to their godfather,' Tim said. 'I have the permit.'

After delivering the boys we drove past the Folly again. The bulldozers were already at work.

'She'll be taken to . . . ?' I hesitated.

'To one of the towers, yes,' Tim said. 'The grief towers for those who refuse to deny. Love is unsocial, inadmissible, contagious.' He grinned. 'It admits communication. Grief for lost love is the worse offence, indictable. It suggests love has value, understanding, generosity, happiness. Tessa is an extreme case. She flaunted her grief with pride.'

'And all personal touches must be erased?' I asked.

'They order it so.' Tim turned onto the motorway. We drove back to my cottage in silence. As we passed the grey lodge we heard strident voices—a party in progress. All the lights outside were on.

'That is encouraged. Safety in numbers ensures isola-tion,' Tim said.

Tim stayed for two more days. We spent them swim-ming, walking, talking, shoring up with friendship the days to come. To some extent we were open to suspicion. Several more inscriptions were torn out of my books. I recognized this mutilation as a hint for me to dispossess myself of personal attachments. I had hidden the letters and the photographs in the disused well in the garden, carefully buried in a steel crate under the bottom bricks. It was destruction of a kind since I could not have them about my house, without resultant loss. Subscribing to current social fashions, I gave a small party, inviting all my neighbours. They all talked at the same time. No one listened to anyone else. No one laughed. Only Tim and I smiled at each other. They felt uneasy because there was no television set. When they left, all together in one group, we played music on the gramophone. It was a small act of defiance. We opened the door to the garden. I wandered out. The tide was coming in. The full moon spotlighted the beach with shifting shafts. The music cast itself like scent in the night air. Tim from indoors waved to me. I faced the direction of the grey lodge. 'Hallo love,' I said, keeping my hand in.

Some movement on the beach caught my attention. Someone was wading out to sea. I smiled, happy that joy had persuaded a swimmer out to a solitary pleasure. I leant on the gate better to see. Someone touched my arm. It was my next door neighbour, the woman. 'Stop him,' she cried. 'Tim,' I shouted and pointed.

Tim ran to the beach. The woman was crying. 'He wouldn't quarrel any more.' I took her indoors. Tim returned, wet, his face sad. 'I'm sorry,' he said to the woman.

'Where are they?' she asked.

'They're taking him to the mortuary,' Tim said.

'I must go to them,' she said.

We tried to stop her.

'They must take me to the tower,' she said. 'It's the only place left for me.' She pushed past Tim. We watched her walk away. We sat in the garden until dawn, looking at the sea. The woman did not return.

'Knew her duty,' said the shopkeeper. 'Sensible. Can't have griefers around. Upsets the tone of the neighbourhood.' She lingered with my change. 'Some should be in as isn't,' she said.

Tim gone, I resumed my daily life, using each hour as positively as I was able. Summer helped to ease the unattended moments which I filled with gardening, long walks, sunbathing and swimming. Night hours were used for work until, tired, I fell into bed and slept. I wrote letters to friends. Sometimes I walked past the grey lodge.

'Still busy?' smirked the shopkeeper.

More towers were built on the coast. At weekends carloads of trippers parked around them. Picnic litter was thrown at their windowless walls, and small boys were encouraged to urinate against them. An elderly man took over the empty cottage next to mine. He ignored all my greetings and sat in his garden sleeping most of the day.

'Harmless now.' The shopkeeper mentioned my new neighbour. 'They emptied him,' she whispered, then gloating, 'Not a memory left!' I paid my bill and left.

'Hallo love,' I said as I returned to my cottage. The old man shifted in his sleep. Indoors my dog barked. There was no one there. There were no more inscriptions to be torn out of any books. I examined everything very carefully: it was all as I had left it. A faint smudge, as of a fingerprint, on Tim's glass panel. It might have been mine. I went to a neighbour's party that evening, passing the grey lodge. The lights were full on, but no sounds came from within. As I returned home I thought I caught a glimpse of somebody in black near my gate. I hurried towards the shadow. I heard footsteps scurry away. Restless, I played game after game of patience until I felt exhausted, although I could not sleep.

'You wasn't working last night,' the shopkeeper said. 'Saw you playing with the cards, all curtains undrawn.' She smirked. 'Not fretting, I hope?'

As autumn drove summer away, my pace of work slackened. I waited for Tim to return. Having no traveller's pass, I was unable to visit other areas. Some ceased to write, those taken to the towers. Such news was hard to contain. During the daytime I increased my show of preoccupation with the commonplace. Only at night, curtains drawn, did I slump into inactivity and anxious imagination. In the mornings I studied my face in the mirror, staring at the signs of strain. I walked along the beach with fretful distress. I dared not pass the grey lodge.

'You look low,' the shopkeeper said.

Like a sparrow deprived of a mate who continues his courting song, thereby attracting the bird of prey, I became insensitive to danger. People stared at me as I passed them without greeting. Belatedly I nodded at their retreating backs. I made some efforts. I planted bulbs, and sat at my desk, writing letters rather than working. I decided to redecorate my cottage: this would indicate that I was not moving towards inaction, and give me an excuse for not adhering to my known routine.

'Picking up again?' The shopkeeper sounded regretful.

I forced myself to walk past the grey lodge once a week. The delivery of mail was reduced to twice weekly, and collection equally restricted. I was asked to several parties and refused the invitations. I pleaded pressure of work. They began to watch me. One morning I ran furiously down the slope to the beach, fell, and twisted my ankle.

'I can express pain now,' I said, as the doctor bound it tight.

'For a fortnight,' he said.

'Does it hurt much?' asked the shopkeeper.

I allowed myself the luxury of going utterly to pieces for forty-eight hours, moving like one demented through the hours, flooding my mind with old memories, meta-phorically wailing at the wall of my loss. Curious neigh-bours called, ostensibly to inquire about my accident. 'The pain,' I said, 'is almost unendurable.' They left satisfied yet doubtful. Through such excess did I propel myself back to an appearance of remoteness. It was a form of subdued hysteria. 'Hallo love,' I said to the morning ending my fortnight of permitted pain. I wondered what part of my anatomy I could next injure without too much damage when I needed the relief of utterance.

'You mustn't get accident-prone,' the doctor said. 'They've read their psychology.' It was a friendly warning.

Tim brought Blanche and Gervase with him from the island. It was a blessing which would see me through the winter. 'We make a group,' Tim said. 'Perfectly acceptable.'

We laughed until tears came.

'We shall go to the grey lodge,' Blanche said.

I experienced relief.

'Not at once,' she said. 'We must move carefully.'

'Visitors, I hear.' The shopkeeper sounded sorry.

Gervase and Tim went for long walks. 'Tower-rubbing', they called it. Gervase would place his hands over the tower walls, palms radiating warmth to the stone. Tim, using a thin chisel, made small penetrations. These were deepened on each visit. In time he reckoned some light would filter through. Blanche urged caution. We heard that Tessa had been taken to the central tower in London for incurables. The old man next door died. The previous tenant, the woman, returned. She did not remember me. They had done a quick job on her: her memory levels were basically superficial.

'She's back to normal now,' said the shopkeeper.

Blanche went to the grey lodge. We waited three hours for her return. Gervase sensed the defeat in her as she came into the room and he rocked her in his arms. I went out to the garden. Tim followed. 'She did not get through.' I wanted to cry forever. 'She went,' Tim said. 'It's a beginning.' When I went back indoors I thanked Blanche for going.

'We must pray for enlightenment,' said Blanche.

The next day Blanche received a letter. She did not show it to me. Gervase delivered her answer to the grey lodge. It was an invitation to go with them when they returned to the island. In the late afternoon I walked along the beach with my dog. A sea mist whirled inland. When I reached the tower Tim was standing outside, back pressed against the stone. Some tension in his stance made me slacken an instinct to run towards him.

'You must go home,' he said. 'At once.'

On the rocks behind him I saw three of them standing, their shapes faintly outlined in the now-thickening fog.

Tim anticipated my question. 'It is permissible to become a voluntary admission.'

'Why?' My voice held terror.

'If one wants to forget,' he said.

My mind took in the implication.

'Blanche thought it likely, possible,' Tim continued, 'that such a solution might come to mind.'

Some joy leapt through my terror. 'That would be some sort of admission.'

'Yes,' Tim said. 'That's why I'm waiting, and why you must go home. There must be no meeting.'

'Waiting?' I lingered on the word. 'Isn't that dangerous? For you?' I glanced at the silent backs stationed on the rocks.

'A risk,' Tim said. 'I'm prepared to take it. I might fail to counter the indecision. An unquiet word might leave no option. The reception committee behind me will see if I fail, and take over. That is the risk.'

As I moved away I heard footsteps, made resonant by the fog, heading towards Tim and the tower. My dog barked a recognition. I hurried on. There were no lights outside or inside the grey lodge. The blinds were pulled up. I went to the shop to buy some cigarettes.

'There's another voluntary,' the shopkeeper said. 'Best to have it out, I always say,' she leered. 'A nice cut-off makes a new person.'

Back at the cottage I saw at once that Blanche knew what was happening.

'We must have faith,' said Gervase, 'and love.'

I closed my eyes and waited for Tim to return.

An hour later Tim came back. 'We're going to the island,' he said. 'We'll start at daybreak.'

There was no need for questions.

'It will not be easy,' Blanche said, 'but it's a break-through, a small mercy.'

'A grace for the living,' said Gervase.

I held Tim's hand until it was time for them to go.

I watched them drive away in the brisk autumn morning light. They took the right fork leading to the grey lodge. There was a touch of frost on the leaves of my roses. The sea splashed tall white waves onto the beach. It was high tide. I turned towards the cottage, and slowly renewed my eyes with every personal aspect. My tension relaxed. There were possibilities. 'Hallo love,' I said, greeting another day.

AFTERWORD

When *They* was first published in 1977, it surely took readers by surprise. Not just because of the eerie, haunting power of the narrative therein, but because it's a complete anomaly in Kay Dick's oeuvre; a surreptitious late-career aberration, the genesis of which is unclear, and whose strangeness never seeps into what she wrote after. Compared to Dick's earlier novels—*By the Lake* (1949), *Young Man* (1951), *An Affair of Love* (1953), *Solitaire* (1958) and *Sunday* (1962), all of which are tales of romantic or familial entanglements set against the backdrop of urbane European settings the writing of which was often praised as "Proustian"—it seems the work of an entirely different writer. Stylistically and tonally, *They* is much closer to the works of experimental British writers Ann Quin—is it just a coincidence that one of the characters is named "Berg," the same as the eponymous protagonist of Quin's 1964 debut?—Christine Brooke-Rose, and Anna Kavan. Dick greatly admired her good friend Brooke-Rose's avant-garde works, especially *Out* (1964), a "race reversal" novel set in the aftermath of a catastrophic event that leaves white people suffering from radiation poisoning, but Black people unscathed. Writing in *Friends and Friendship* (1974), her collection of interviews with fellow authors, Dick described the novel as "powerful, sinister, near prophetic . . . Orwellian fiction." While *Ice* (1967), Kavan's enigmatic, almost psychedelic final novel—in which a man pursues a silver-haired woman across a snowy, post-apocalyptic wasteland—reads like a sinister dream sequence, a description that could also be applied to the unsettling, cryptic chapters of *They*. Interestingly, both Brooke-Rose and Kavan switched registers following episodes of significant upheaval in their lives. The former survived a near-fatal kidney operation in 1962, while Kavan's midlife reinvention has been much mythologized: "Once a wholesome young English housewife who wrote conventional women's fiction, so the story goes, in her thirties she was confined to an insane asylum and emerged as a chic, emaciated bottle-blonde heroin addict, wielding a bleak and anarchic new literary voice," summarized the critic Emma Garman. Whether *They* was the result of something similar in Dick's life, we can't be sure. She certainly underwent a period of intense bereavement and loss in the 1960s—this included the breakdown of a relationship, followed by the death of a lover who killed herself, an experience Dick later wrote about in her final novel, *The Shelf* (1984), and a suicide attempt of her own, which she talks about in the autobiographical essay included in *Friends and Friendship*. These experiences could also explain her particular interest in "Coping with Grief," the 1975 *Sunday Times* article that she takes such pains to credit at the beginning of *They*. What we do know for sure, though, is that in *Friends and Friendship* Dick points out that what makes Brooke-Rose's most recent writing "so remarkable" is its "divergence . . . from her earlier more fashionable novels." Perhaps her admiration for such an astonishing volte-face—combined with the impact of the recent emotional disturbances she'd undergone—inspired Dick to try something similar herself. After all, she writes "Hallo Love," the final chapter of *They*, only a year later, in March 1975.

Aptly, much of the novel's power lies in its various mysteries. There's the enigmatic "They," "omnipresent and elusive," as Philip Howard describes them in his review in *The Times*, dangerous and violent, but also strangely vacant and automaton-like. That they're an informal multitude, rather than a government-sanctioned group like Ray Bradbury's book-burning "firemen" in *Fahrenheit 451* (1953) or George Orwell's all-pervading government surveillance in *Nineteen Eighty-Four* (1949), makes Dick's creations all the more ominous. Their initial strength lies not in official mandates, but rather in the swell of their ever-increasing numbers. Rarely distinguished as individuals, they're situated in stark contrast to the narrator and the other artists, intellectuals and craftspeople.

There is a certain degree of inscrutability here, too, though. In neither naming the narrator, nor revealing their gender, *They* is Dick's most radically androgynous book. In a 1986 interview with Kris Kirk published in *The Guardian*, Dick explained that the "overall tone" of the personal relationships depicted in her books is always bisexual, as this is how she herself identified. Although sexually attracted to both men and women, she described there being "something extra"—"this love, this emotion"—in her relationships with the latter, but she was in any case uninterested in binaries. "I have certain prejudices and one of them is that I cannot bear apartheid of any kind—class, colour or sex," she continues. "Gender is of no bloody account."

So who was this wonderfully outspoken, confident woman? The more I discover about her life, a figure emerges who is just as singular and trailblazing as her remarkable novel. Dick was born to an unmarried mother in London in 1915. "She must have had great courage," writes Dick in *Friends and Friendship*, "because illegitimacy in the First World War was a very unpleasant business to be mixed up with, especially for a woman brought up in a reasonably privileged fashion." Her mother had already broken with her more respectable family before she became pregnant with Dick, instead making her home among the bohemian society that revolved around London's famous Café Royal—"artists, actresses, *demi-mondaines*—penniless the lot of them," as Dick describes the crowd—and this is where Dick's mother immediately returned when she was discharged from the hospital with her newborn daughter. After such a "baptism"—Dick received no religious ceremony, just the "toasts and blessings" that were exchanged by the Royal's patrons over her head on her first night on earth—it's "small wonder that I have a taste for café life," she explains.

The childhood that followed was cosmopolitan and distinctly European; travels on the Continent were de rigueur. From the age of four, she and her mother were kept by her mother's lover, a wealthy Swiss man who eventually left his wife and married Dick's mother when Dick was seven, thus transforming their "stateless merriment" into "middle-class respectable living." A two-year stint at an expensive English girls' boarding school proved unpleasant, so Dick was sent to a coed day school in Geneva instead (she lodged with a local family), an experience she found much more agreeable, and thereafter she finished her education at the Lycée Français de Londres in South Kensington.

Dick recalls having known, since the age of ten, that she wanted to become a writer. "There was never any doubt in my mind," she explains in *Friends and Friendship*. But as her stepfather had lost some of his money by the time she came of age, sitting in an ivory tower wasn't an option. Not that the prospect of earning her own living perturbed her. Dick began her "career in the book trade," as she puts it, and thus found herself "back with those penniless bohemians of the Café Royal." When talking to Kirk, she recalls frequenting the gay bars and cafés of London's Soho, which she and her bisexual friend Tony gadded about together, both wearing cloaks and carrying walking sticks. "I ran to the artists and writers we'd now call the Alternative Society," she explains. "We were very politically motivated, the Spanish Civil War was our Mecca." After various editorial jobs, she became—at the tender age of twenty-six—the first woman director in English publishing, at P. S. King & Son, after which she was made the editor (under the pen name Edward Lane) of the short-lived but acclaimed literary periodical *The Windmill*: it was she who commissioned and then published, in the magazine in 1946, Orwell's now famous essay in defence of P. G. Wodehouse.

During the mid-twentieth century, Dick was at the very heart of the London literary scene. A list of the guests regularly entertained by her and her partner, the novelist Kathleen Farrell, at their Hampstead home at 55 Flask Walk—they lived together from 1940 to 1962—includes a host of successful and popular writers of the era, including C. P. Snow, Pamela Hansford Johnson, Brigid Brophy, Muriel Spark, Stevie Smith, Olivia Manning, Angus Wilson, and Francis King. For a woman who regarded her friends so highly, the obituary that ran in *The Guardian* on the occasion of Dick's death in 2001, age eighty-six, did her an unforgiveable disservice. Its author, the writer and journalist Michael De-la-Noy, claims that Dick "expended far more energy in pursuing personal vendettas and romantic lesbian friendships than in writing books"—a cutthroat accusation that smacks of a vendetta all its own. Unbelievably, he then goes on to describe Dick as a failed artist, "a talented woman bedeviled by ingratitude and a kind of manic desire to avenge totally imaginary wrongs." Although this was wild enough to grab my attention when I first came across the obituary, it soon became clear, after only the most cursory of further investigations, that De-la-Noy's defamatory assertions couldn't be further from the truth.

"Here is a writer who respects human beings even in their pettiness or confusion; who regards each of them as a worthy object of study and even tenderness, and who devotes as much space and care to the description of what one might call a thoroughly trivial person as to a creature of heroic design," wrote *The Sphere*'s critic Vernon Fane in his review of Dick's second novel, *Young Man. Sunday*—a loosely auto-biographical story about Dick's childhood and her relationship with her mother—goes even further in demonstrating its author's psychological astuteness; reviewing the novel for the *Daily Telegraph*, Peter Green extolled Dick's "positively Proustian nose for significant nuances of behaviour."

So uncharitable were De-la-Noy's awful charges, *The Guardian* received letters of rebuttal from many of Dick's closest friends. The writer of one of these, the author and journalist Roy Greenslade, who was a neighbour of Dick's in Brighton for thirty years, was adamant that any of the "silly feuds" she indulged in were far "outweighed by her acts of kindness and generosity towards her friends, especially young people. She encouraged almost every youngster she ever met to write, lauding their efforts to the skies in public, while offering helpful criticism in private." The author Michael Ratcliffe also defended his friend passionately: "Kay was funny, encouraging and generous," he writes. "The young loved her, and she them." This side of her character is completely absent in De-la-Noy's obituary, but clearly it's one of the things that those who knew Dick valued most highly. As Greenslade continues:

> She was, in fact, a most perceptive critic, preferring too often to spend her time reading the works of others rather than writing herself. Few people read as much as Kay. "Darling, I've just been rereading Scott," she once said. "He was brilliant." I asked: "Which novel?" "All of them," she replied, without the least sign of boasting. Her other great talent lay in introducing people she met to her wide network of friends and contacts. She loved our children, helped them, made them laugh, made them think. Both of them, like my wife and I, benefited from

knowing the lady with the cigarette holder and the succession of dogs along the terrace.

Pertinently though, Ratcliffe expresses his confidence that "[p]osterity will place her work." And now, twenty years on, he's been proved right.

Little did I know, when I first wrote about *They* for the *Paris Review Daily* in August 2020, that within less than a year I would have the chance to bring it back into print with McNally Editions. The Dick I've discovered is an utterly beguiling woman, one who, although undoubtedly spiky, produced a large body of important work while also living an extremely full, free life in the company of many dear friends. *Pierrot* (1960), for example, her study of commedia dell'arte, is considered something of a definitive work on the subject. Then, during the fifteen-year gap between *Sunday* and *They*, she published two absorbing volumes of literary interviews: *Ivy and Stevie* (1971) and the aforementioned *Friends and Friendship*. Writing in *The Times* in 1974, A. S. Byatt declares that the former "would always be required reading" for anyone interested in either of its subjects, Ivy Compton-Burnett and Stevie Smith. Dick's later obituary in the same newspaper attributes her success as an interlocutor to the fact that she was a woman of "sympathy and perception," one who'd "persuaded two naturally reticent women writers . . . to reveal more about their inner lives than they had ever done to anyone, except obliquely through their writings." My great hope is that this reissue of *They* will not only reintroduce this brilliant novel to the world, but that it will also go some considerable way to setting the record straight when it comes to its author's character and achievements. As Paul Bailey avowed in *The Observer*, her autobiographical portrait in *Friends and Friendship* reveals "a most interesting and complex woman, a woman worth reading about." He describes Dick's writing as "poignant, honest, occasionally catty, and—finally—extremely sympathetic."

Through the 1940s and '50s, although clearly already an accomplished editor—Orwell, for example, inscribed Dick's copy of *Animal Farm* (1945) with "Kay—To make it and me acceptable" in recognition of her editorial work— as a writer, she was still learning her craft. But it's in the latter half of her career—by which point Dick had left London and moved to Brighton, and had campaigned tirelessly for the Public Lending Rights Bill, which, when it was passed in 1979, finally allowed authors to receive payment for the free loan of their books through the UK public library system—that she comes into her own as a novelist: first with *They*, and thereafter *The Shelf*, which is written as a letter to Francis King, and relates the story of the brief affair Dick had with a married woman in the early 1960s—not long after the breakdown of her relationship with Farrell—and this lover's tragic suicide. The events she described are true, Dick tells Kirk, before adding mischievously, "Though I shall deny it, of course."

There's truth to be found in *They* too, despite the distractions of its dystopian, experimental elements. Yes, it reminds us of the value of art and culture, but it's also a book about the importance of friends; it's a fictional exposition of this impassioned cry, in *Friends and Friendship*, for what Dick most holds dear: "I shall never wish to stop rereading the books I love, looking at paintings, listening to music, and, more than that, I should wish to know my friends forever." Like any strong allegory, *They* can be read many ways—as a straightforward satire, a sequence of vividly-drawn nightmares, even a metaphor for artistic struggle—but above all, it's perhaps best understood as a plea for individual and intellectual freedoms made by an artist who refused to live by many of society's rules. As Dick herself reminds us, "it is an extremely courageous act to be a writer, painter, composer, because you are out on your own, in limbo, totally unprotected, not much encouraged, driven only by some inner conviction and strength, and the discipline is yours alone."

Lucy Scholes
London, 2021